LIFESPAN OF STARLIGHT

LIFESPAN OF STAR LIGHT

THALIA KALKIPSAKIS

hardie grant EGMONT

Lifespan of Starlight
published in 2015 by
Hardie Grant Egmont
Ground Floor, Building 1, 658 Church Street
Richmond, Victoria 3121, Australia
www.hardiegrantegmont.com.au

A CiP record for this title is available from the National Library of Australia

Text copyright © 2015 Thalia Kalkipsakis
Text design copyright © 2015 Hardie Grant Egmont
Cover design by Design by Committee
Typeset in Bembo 11/17pt by Cannon Typesetting

1 3 5 7 9 10 8 6 4 2

Printed in Australia by Griffin Press, an Accredited ISO AS/NZS
14001:2004 Environmental Management System printer.

FSC
www.fsc.org
MIX
Paper from
responsible sources
FSC® C009448

The paper this book is printed on is certified against Forest
Stewardship Council® Standards. Griffin Press holds FSC
chain of custody certification SGS-COC-005088. FSC
promotes environmentally responsible, socially beneficial
and economically viable management of the world's forests.

Life can only be understood backwards;
but it has to be lived forwards.

Søren Kierkegaard

To Campbell

CHAPTER ONE

JUST STEPPING OFF the curb takes all the courage I have. An intake of air and I bail out, my toes gripping the soles of my boots for all I'm worth and the rest of me teetering over the edge. A car flashes past and I jump back. That was close.

From a distance comes the high-pitched hum of another one. But from which direction? These stupid smartcars are so fast; you're still registering that one is coming when it's already on top of you. The hum rises in pitch until, *voom*. A flash of metal and the rush of air. Right to left.

I make a note. That's the sound I'll need to recognise if I'm going to make it across. But then, another. *Voom*. The same hum, except this one is left to right. I didn't pick the difference.

Come on, Scout. You can do it. But still I don't move. Instead I check over my shoulder in case someone's coming who will trigger the crossing point for me. During the day that's all it would take. Just hang around until someone walks up. But it's late now, after ten, and who would be heading over to the park at this hour? For a start, it's locked.

My fists clench, trying to muster the strength, a barrier maybe against those speeding metal bullets. Another car zooms past. This is so stupid.

I'm going to die.

I could make it across easy if I had my compad, though by 'my' I really mean Mum's old one. Calling it my lifeline is no understatement. I've set up a shortcut that triggers a crossing point the same as if I were chipped, complete with a cleanup bot that removes any trace of me hacking into the system.

But the compad is still sitting in a dock next to the door at home. In my anger, I didn't grab it on my way out like I normally do automatically. But even when I realised I didn't have it, I couldn't go back. Not after what I'd said to Mum.

I don't need your help anymore, all right? I can handle it on my own …

Even the memory of it makes me cringe. She actually did a double-take when I said that, she was so surprised. Disappointed, maybe, too. But even after all that Mum's done for me, all that she's given up, I still wasn't expecting her to suggest what she did.

The memory of our argument lifts my resolve, as if crossing the road is a way to prove that I *can* handle it all on my own. To Mum, but also to myself.

There's just the small matter of working out how.

When I next pick a car in the distance, I count under my breath until it flashes past. Three cats-and-dogs. That means three seconds is the time I'll have to bolt across two lanes to the centre of the road. Could I do that? Maybe.

I just have to go for it, I decide.

One foot in front of the other, arms ready, a sprinter at the starting line: my eyes focus on the raised median strip in the middle of the road. It seems so close.

Another car flashes past, left to right. As soon as it's out of earshot, my ears buzz with the strain of listening for more hums.

None.

So I bolt. Across two empty lanes to my island refuge in the centre of the road. Panting, but safe. Too easy. I feel stupid to have waited so long.

An alarm sounds, and I realise my mistake. It must have a movement sensor set up to detect stray dogs that might wander onto the road. The screech of it fills my mind with blind panic. This is bad. Can't let them see I'm *not* a dog. The next thing I know I'm sprinting across the final two lanes, my only thought to escape any traffic cameras.

At the back of it all, I also hear another sound – a high-pitched hum drawing closer. A smartcar is coming straight at me.

I turn to see the approaching lights as I run, and in that split second the whole world seems to stall. Each moment feels like a million, everything happening in slow motion.

As soon as my foot touches the curb, everything snaps back to normal. The alarm goes quiet, but as the car passes, I get this flash of some guy who's just glanced up from his screen, his mouth in a zero as he sees that it was *me* on the road.

This basically sums up the story of my life: stuck on the outside, looking in. A stray on the edge of society.

I cringe and do this awkward wave that's meant to mean: *my mistake* … But the car is gone before the guy has time to react. I don't hang around, just head straight for my gap in the fence and slip through into Footscray Park. Made it.

Here at least, there's somewhere I can relax. If you cut across the garden bed near the main entrance you'll come to a section of retaining wall that has crumbled, collapsing in on itself to form a broad cave. Inside, the walls are damp from the trickle of an underground spring that must have washed away soil and mortar over the years. Lucky for me you can't see a thing from the path because the whole lot is hidden behind spiky bushes and the thick trunk of a ghost gum.

I discovered the cave years ago when I was hiding from a park council worker after scooping a bucket of water from the Maribyrnong Canal. He didn't bother chasing me, of course. He didn't need to. He just triggered an alarm on his compad to alert the police. Then he looked for my chip on the grid so he could tag it with a crim suspect stamp.

What the park council worker didn't know, unhappily for him, is that I'm illegal which means I'm not chipped. My wrist is as smooth as the day I was born. The only reason I'm alive is that Mum bribed her GP into signing a form saying that she'd had an abortion. So all I had to do when the council worker triggered the alarm was find a half-decent hiding place and I was totally off-grid.

I didn't want to lose any water from the bucket by running so I did this weird sort of speed walk, taking care to hold the bucket high and in both hands. I even remember glancing over my shoulder and calling 'sorry' as I escaped up the path because, you know, even though I'm illegal I'm not a bad person.

The guy didn't even look up though. He just kept frowning at his compad, not getting it at all, wasting time tapping at his screen before he realised that in order to catch me he had to actually watch where I went. I was only planning to crouch behind those spiky bushes but once I did, I discovered the cave, complete with underground spring.

I haven't had to steal from the canal since then. The water is achingly cold and tastes faintly of moss, way better than anything that comes out of the potable tap in our room. But it's not just thirst that draws me to the cave tonight.

I need space to think.

The first thing I notice as I duck into the cave is that my picnic blanket has been moved. Lately I've been spending more time in here and I've stashed a few things away. Blanket. Water container. Pocketknife and hand shovel from when I tried to grow potatoes and failed.

There's not much moonlight to see by, but my eyes adjust quickly. As they do, I freeze. The blanket has been moved because someone is *lying* under it.

Slowly I back away, ready to run. For all I know, the woman under the blanket is a council worker in disguise. I'm almost out of the cave when something changes about the woman.

Maybe it's a play of shadows, but her frame appears to flicker, as if she's a hologram or something. Even though I'm not sure what just happened, it's enough to make me stop.

When she comes into focus again, the woman breathes in quickly, her cracked lips lifting gently at the corners. Her face is so far out of step with the state of her body that still I just stare. She's little more than a bag of bones, way skinnier than I am. One cheek is cracked and bleeding. And yet, her expression …

It's complete and utter bliss.

I stumble forwards and drop to my knees, reaching for her hand and then pulling back when I see two of its fingers are swollen and black. My hand lands on a bony shoulder instead.

'Are you all right?' I ask, which is about the dumbest thing anyone could say because clearly she is anything but all right.

Her eyes shift my way but her only response is to pant.

'I'll call for help. Where's your compad?' I lift the blanket to search then drop it after an eyeful of skin and a whole face full of stale sweat stink. Fantastic. The woman is naked and the number of compads between the two of us is a sum total of zero.

'Listen,' I lean closer, trying not to breathe in her stench. How do I explain to her that I don't have my compad? It's like trying to tell her that I forgot to bring my left arm. 'I have to go and get help, okay? I'll come back …' I say it loudly, as if making the words clear will somehow help her understand.

She turns my way slowly as if only now aware I'm here, so I try again. 'I'll go and get help, okay?'

Her smile – that strange expression of bliss – fades slightly and her lips part to let out the faintest breath. 'No.'

'Listen, I left my compad at home. I have no way to get help. I have to go –'

'No,' she manages again, firmer this time. Then, still weak, 'Please. *Stay.*'

Every cell in my brain is telling me this woman needs to be in hospital. Even the smell about her is wrong. The stench of death. But she keeps her eyes on me as if waiting for my response, a promise. And so I tuck one foot under my butt, terrified of what I'm saying. 'Okay. I'm here.'

Her eyes track away from me once I say that. She seems to concentrate on something, her breathing slow and deliberate. I hold onto the sound.

I'm not sure how long we stay that way but it feels like ages. Each second draws out longer than the last. We reach a point when her breathing changes, seems to fade and almost stop, and I find myself watching her chest for movement.

After a while I begin to wonder whether she's even aware that I'm here. Maybe I could sneak away and call for help. But something keeps me. She wanted me to stay, and even though there's a difference between what she wants and what she needs, I keep my promise. Maybe because I know better than anyone how it feels to be alone. Or maybe because part of me knows I wouldn't make it back in time.

At one point I think I hear a sigh, though perhaps it's just a gust of wind.

I don't pick the exact moment, but there comes a time when I realise that she isn't breathing anymore. We barely shared more than a few sentences but the sense of loss settles around me like a mist. The woman asked me to stay; now she's the one who has gone.

For a long time I stay like that, by her side. It's only when dawn light starts to shine dimly through the mouth of the cave that I move stiffly, reaching out to lift the blanket over her face. One arm is resting across her stomach on top of the blanket so I hesitate, deciding whether to move the arm beneath the blanket as well or leave her as she is.

In the early morning light I can clearly see a single line about a centimetre long on the back of her wrist — the telltale scar where a chip was inserted, the mark of a citizen.

I find myself staring at it as an idea snakes inside me. If I hadn't argued with Mum last night, I might never have thought of this. Part of me is shocked at myself for even considering it.

But another, more determined part of me knows that when the time comes, I'll do it.

Our argument last night began with yet another dance around the last chunk of bread.

Mum started it. 'You have it, Scout.'

'No, no. It's all yours.' My usual response.

We were sitting in front of the comscreen, plates in our laps, picking through news segments that wouldn't put us off our food. Already I'd scrolled past a famine crisis overseas, as well as a massive fire in central New South Wales. I skipped over two war reports without pausing. There's always loads of stuff on about the war in East Asia.

'Please. I want you to have it.' Mum placed the chunk on my plate but I shook my head and dropped it back on hers without taking my eyes off the screen.

Mum's a federal citizen, chipped and everything. She's tertiary qualified too, which means she gets full C-grade rations – more than enough food for a woman her size and enough second-level water for a shower every other day. It's the sort of lifestyle that many people would envy I guess, especially if you compare it to someone on school leaver's rations. But split Mum's rations in two, for her and her illegal teenage daughter, and suddenly there's barely enough. Water used to be our main problem, but since I found the underground spring, food has taken over as our scarcest resource.

'Coutlyn, please. Take it,' Mum said, her voice rising.

I glanced over at her and shook my head, the insistence in her tone only making me more determined.

'You're *not* hungry?' she asked incredulously.

Of course I was hungry. I always am. I don't care what anyone says, you never get used to it. The deep hollowness that is never filled, and the constant tiredness, nobody could get used to that. But our conversation wasn't really about hunger; it wasn't even about food.

As if it's not enough to know how much Mum had to give up in order to keep me, every day I also have to see her fade a little more because she shares her food rations with me. The older I've grown, the skinnier she's become. Seeing that does strange things to your mind.

When Mum finally realised I wasn't going to take the last chunk of bread, she let out a long sigh and clicked her fingers to switch the comscreen channel.

Of all things to bring up, it was an ad about treatments that speed the recovery of chip scars on the wrists of newborns.

I couldn't help a snort at one of the words they kept repeating: *unsightly*. Where do they get off?

'What do you think?' Mum asked once the ad was over.

A shrug. 'Each to their own.'

'I've been saving up.'

'You're worried about your chip scar?' I didn't get her meaning at first.

'No.' And she said it so bluntly, so cleanly, that I knew what she was going to say before she'd even said it, knew it like a freight train charging right at me:

'I've been saving up for you.'

Now that I thought about it, I realised she'd been dropping hints for weeks. Scary stuff about the way adult illegals are treated, and how important it is for me to register in the education system if I'm to have any chance of landing a job. But honestly, despite the looming registration date for the select-entry test, I hadn't seen this coming.

Mum wanted to give me her chip, transfer her citizenship to me, so I could finally go to school.

'You can't have a fresh scar as a fourteen-year-old,' said Mum.

Already I was shaking my head. 'No way.'

'Listen.' Mum flicked off the comscreen and leaned forward in her chair. 'We already survive on one person's rations. Nothing has to change except you'll be the one who's chipped.'

'No, Mum.'

'It's your turn now, understand? I've been reading up, it's a simple procedure. Nothing has to change.'

'No.' How many times did I have to say it? 'You can't even *get* to work without your chip. That's not even an option. I can sort it out some other way.'

'How, Scout? Registration for the test closes in five days.'

'I'll still register with your chip, okay? There is no difference because it's going to stay in your wrist. Where it belongs.'

'And then they'll map me going to work when you're meant to be going to school?'

'No. I'm going to fix that.'

'How, Scout? How? You really want to risk them finding out you're illegal? Once you register in the school system you won't be off-grid anymore. You realise how much more dangerous that will be?'

'You want to start lecturing *me* about being off-grid?' I yelled. The tone in her voice was scaring me. 'I'm the one who has to live with it every day, okay? I'm the one who knows what it's like. Not you!'

Thinking back, I hate the way that must have sounded. How ungrateful must she think I am? I tried to soften my tone. 'Even something as simple as crossing the street is hard. You realise that?' I said carefully.

'Okay,' Mum was already nodding. 'Then teach me. What do I have to do? I'm going to have to learn –'

But the idea of Mum out there without a chip stuck right in my heart. Before I could stop myself, I stood up and let the frustration fly.

'No you won't, because I won't take your chip! Never! I don't need your help anymore, all right? I can handle it on my own.'

That's when I stormed out.

In the cool morning light, I make my way up the ramp that leads out of Footscray Park.

The park isn't open yet, so I duck out the same way I came in. I reach the crossing point on Ballarat Road, swipe and wait.

Just a girl. Crossing a road.

Nothing happens at first. *Voom*. Left to right. And then another. Way busier than last night. For a moment I wonder if maybe it's not going to work, but then I hear the familiar drop in tone as smartcars are brought to a stop in both directions.

Then there's a ping and a green light, just for me. Just for standing here.

My breath sounds too loud as I cross. The people in the cars wouldn't even bother to glance up, but I feel as if they're watching me. My fingertips press the chip hard into my palm so there's no chance of losing it. It's sticky, still fleshy, and in a gruesome way I'm glad, because I don't want to forget where it came from. I'm carrying part of that woman with me, even as I leave her behind.

Before I do anything, I'll need to hack into the system and clean off as much of her life as I can. Some things are set, but most records can be changed. When I'm done they'll have no way of tracing her chip to me, even if they find her body.

When I make it to the other side, I break into a run because I can't wait to see the look on Mum's face when I tell her:

See? Told you I'd handle it. Everything's going to be okay.

CHAPTER TWO

I ROLL OVER AND sigh at the empty space beside me. Shouldn't have let myself doze off. Mum didn't stir when I burst in earlier, so I slipped in beside her, planning to lie here until she woke. When I check the time it's even later than I thought; Mum would have left an hour ago.

Groggily, I tap around on the upturned box beside the bed until my fingertips touch the chip. It's still there, tucked out of sight between the lamp and the wall.

I hitch myself up on an elbow and examine the chip in my palm, feeling the weird sense again of that woman here with me.

I'll make this count for something, I say silently. *Promise.*

Carefully I wipe it on an old rag, trying not to touch it any more than I have to. Then I slip it inside my boot, beneath the lining, aware even as I do that there's no point hiding it. The grid would have mapped the chip making its way from the park to here.

Mum's typed a message on my compad: *Left you an egg. We'll talk tonight. Much love.*

Immediately, I hit reply. She can't talk on the phone at work so I message her terminal. *Call me if you can? I have something to tell you.*

The reply comes back in seconds. *You OK? I have clients all day.*

Yeah, I type and then I go blank, staring at the screen. How do I explain what happened? It's a risk to say anything in a compad message anyway; the authorities are all over these things once they find a reason to go looking. In the end I just type: *I'm OK. See you tonight.*

I cook the egg on a stovetop in the corner of our room, aware that this will be the last time I eat food that should have been Mum's. She'll need most of her water rations so I take only a few mouthfuls from the potable tap. I could swipe the sensor with that woman's chip, of course, but I don't want to risk that until I've cleaned her deets.

The comscreen flickers to life. Let's see who we're dealing with here.

First up, I run a bot that moves the screen through a set of news sites, automatically selecting random links. It used to run on a continuous loop, but then Alistair taught me how to code it for random clicks, which makes it much more lifelike.

Alistair lives in the room next to ours and he taught me everything I know about computers. He's ninety-one years old, and is as close to a genius as anyone I've met. Most people his age have been forced to retire, which means only G-level rations, but he's been on AA-level for years, way higher than Mum. No matter how many different ways I ask, he still won't tell me what job he does.

I let the bot run for a while to make sure it's working, watching fake-me scroll through the extreme weather alerts for today. Security would have to be pretty smart to pick that it's not a person browsing. Maybe a person with attention deficit disorder, but still.

While the bot keeps running, I hack into the back end of the system and set up a smokescreen to hide the fact I'm back here. Alistair describes this bit as sort of scuffing dirt over a path to hide your tracks.

Now, I bring up the grid.

A map of our street comes up with every person here pinpointed as a single bright dot. Normal citizens aren't meant to be able to see this. Out of habit I check for Kessa and her twin sister in the house at the end of our street, but no-one is there of course; they'd be at school and their parents at work. Two dots come up for Mr and Mrs Richardson in our front room after the late shift last night; and, for the first time, I find one in our room that's not Mum.

I stare, mesmerised by the dot. It's strange to have wished so hard for something all my life and feel so weird now that I have it. I guess because it's not mine, really. And because of the way I got it. I shudder, suppressing the memory.

Now I layer a history map over the top and the street becomes a 3D grid. Instead of dots, long worms stretch back from each person in 3D, mapping the paths they've taken to reach their current location. It's possible to track back in time to see a snapshot of where everyone was on, say, Christmas morning. Or any time you like.

You can pretty much track entire lives in reverse, at least as far back as when they first received their chip. You can access other stuff too, like ration points, health records, job history. Alistair says names and birth certificates are kept in a separate place because of privacy laws, but it's pretty easy to work out who is who from the other information.

Before I clear out the woman's deets, I want to check out her history map. She looked like a homeless woman, and sure smelled like one, but I can't help wondering whether someone might want to know what happened to her. I owe her that much. Once I wipe her past, she'll pretty much disappear from the grid.

I track back my own history map since I've been holding the chip, along the streets of Footscray, crossing Ballarat Road this morning and then back to last night and the park. She must have found the underground spring around six o'clock …

And there, I stop. Or rather the *worm* stops, which doesn't make sense. It's as if someone's already wiped the history map clean. Either that or at six o'clock last night the woman suddenly appeared out of thin air.

I lean back in the armchair, staring at the empty grid, trying to work out what's going on. Maybe it's just a glitch. So I pull out of the mainframe and then hack back in to see if that fixes the problem.

Instead of tracking backwards from now, I type in the date and time: last night at six o'clock.

There it is again, a dead end. For a while I scroll around the park at a few minutes before six, trying to find the woman again, but it's hard to pick up a history map when I've lost the thread.

Still not sure what's going on, I check out her ration points. Maybe I can track her by the delivery locations. The ration points are low level, but good enough for someone my age and the best thing is, she hasn't accessed them. Not even water.

I spend time tracking back her ration points, trying to see when she last accessed them and finding nothing. Maybe she was surviving on rubbish scraps or something, because her points are complete for months. Or perhaps her chip was malfunctioning and she never did anything about it.

For a while I just stare at the screen with my nose scrunched, deciding whether it's okay to feel pleased about what I've found. Or rather what I *haven't* found, because it seems there's no need to worry about anyone noticing that the woman's gone; according to the grid it's as if she barely existed in the first place.

The job history is blank, and her school records only go as far as junior school, which can't be right. Her chip must have been glitchy, that's the only way to explain this. Plus the insertion stamp is too recent for her age, so maybe this is a replacement chip.

A sharp sigh, and I make a decision. I set about wiping all her deets anyway. Maybe I can use the glitch if I'm ever questioned. *It's the chip that's the problem, not me.*

With her deets cleared, I start adding my own: the grades I would have been given if I'd been going to school, my date of birth, health records, adding the things that would have been recorded by my chip if I'd been a real citizen. Making myself legit in reverse. I'm expecting the glitch to cause gaps and deletions like it did for the woman, but it all works fine.

Finally, once I've added all I can, I shut down the session in the mainframe. When the front screen comes up I see I've been busy reading about a train crash in India, just outside the war zone. So I switch off the bot, and regain control of the front end. The real me, this time. Then I click through to the central website for all the select-entry high schools and hit 'register'.

An alert comes up warning that registration for the select-entry test will cost 550 energy rations, which I didn't expect, but since the woman had a full quota saved, it's not a problem.

Then it flashes for a swipe request. I'm expecting I'll have to take the chip out of my boot, but first I try swiping the sole.

I hear it, for the second time this morning: a ping. Application accepted. The date for the entry test comes up: ten days from now, already added to 'my' diary for convenience. All I need bring to the test, it tells me, is a pencil and eraser. And a chip hidden in the lining of my boot.

I sleep for a little while longer, but it's not long before my eyes zap open. Why waste the day in bed when I can do so many things? A haircut in a real salon, a ride on the fast train. But before I do anything else, I'm ticking off my number one.

It takes me a few tries before I actually make it into a cafe. The first two I pass, my legs just keep walking, as if they simply can't believe I'm allowed to join the end of the queue.

Finally, I reach a small cafe near the overpass with no-one waiting outside and a couple of spare tables near the back. I make my way to the counter as a woman with spiky blue hair passes a table number to the guy in front of me. She looks my way and raises her eyebrows.

'Three hundred mil of water, please.' I clamp my mouth shut, waiting for something to happen, an alarm to sound or something.

'Anything else?'

Such a simple question. 'Maybe a ...' My eyes flit over the cakes and muffins on display on the counter. 'What are those?' I ask, pointing. It comes out quietly.

'Cornbread muffins.'

'One of those, please?' I ask, half-expecting her to tell me I've ordered too much. But she keys it all in without blinking. The woman gestures towards a compad on the counter as it flashes up the cost: 300 points potable water, 513 points food.

A simple swipe of my wrist past the receiver, my hand in a fist to hide the chip pressed between my palm and a finger, and there's a ping.

Transaction approved.

The taste of the muffin makes my brain melt. It's like the flavour of all the meals I've ever eaten, all at once, in one bite of muffin. But halfway through it, a wave of nausea washes over me and I realise that if I keep eating I might see it all again. I sip the water in between bites but it's not long before I have to stop. I shuffle back in the chair.

How insane. Half a glass of water and half a muffin sit in front of me. I'm so used to having half and only half of everything that I seem to have a barrier against eating more. I suddenly wish that Mum were here now, sharing with me. Except this time, I'd be giving half my rations to her.

The other people sitting at tables are mostly adults, washing down sandwiches with the latest coffee concentrate. A couple of guys in Murdoch High School uniforms are getting stuck into the biggest triangles of orange cake I've ever seen, and I find myself calculating how many illegals they could accept into the city if they cut back citizen rations by maybe 300 points each day.

There are more like me, of course, mostly living outside the city limits: other single mums like mine who couldn't bear to lose their babies, people who campaigned against the ration system, or are too ill to work. They're not exiled, exactly; it's more that without access to water and food rations, they're forced to go looking. Anywhere but here.

It feels wrong to leave anything to waste, so I force myself to finish the glass of water. Then I wrap up the remains of the muffin and take it home with me.

It's not long until Mum's due back so I get busy ordering food for tonight – veg sausages, mushrooms, real butter. I still have a whole 80 points of my daily maximum left once I've hit the final order so I blow them on a fresh orange, all the way from northern New South Wales. It costs 50 credits on top of the ration points because of transport costs, and I have this pang at the extravagance.

Just this once, I promise myself. We have reason to celebrate.

As soon as I hear the ping from the delivery drone, I dash out to the front chute in bare feet.

Mrs Richardson must have been waiting for her delivery too. She steps out of her door at the same time as me, immediately looking away when she sees me.

'Hey! How are you, Mrs Richardson?' It's a bit immature, but I can't help it. Mum hates it when I do this.

'Yes, hello,' she mumbles without making eye contact. I hang back while she selects her package and shuffles towards the kitchen. She's always worried, I think, that I'll ask to share her rations, but Mum and I have always coped on our own. And anyway, we already owe the Richardsons enough for keeping quiet all these years.

When Mum moved here I was a few months old, just a single woman and her baby. The Richardsons were really kind at first. I think they must have felt sorry for her. In their minds, the only way that Mum could be a single mum would be if Dad had died.

It took a few years before they realised that wasn't true. I still remember the first time Mrs Richardson turned away after I'd called out to her in the hallway. As if I didn't exist. It was around the time that I was due to start school. They must have worked out that if I wasn't going to school, I wasn't chipped.

The truth is that my father's an Egyptian national who was working here as a tactical specialist when he met Mum. But once he'd trained the local staff, they cancelled his visa, citing limited resources. It didn't matter that Mum was pregnant by then, or that he faced persecution from his own government because of the work he did here.

Now we can't find any record of him at all, but Mum still clings to the hope that he escaped detection when he returned and is living underground. We can't search for him too often because of what it would mean for us all if we were found out.

Our evening delivery is way fatter than usual tonight. Heavy. I pull it out of the chute and carry it proudly to our room. Alistair and the Richardsons use the big share kitchen to prepare their meals, but Mum installed a small stovetop and sink in our room years ago so our split ration sizes aren't obvious to everyone else in the house.

The veg sausages are sizzling nicely when Mum comes home from work. She makes a questioning sound and frowns at the pan. 'Hold on, there must be a mistake.'

'No mistake.' I make a big show of dropping mushrooms into the pan then lift *a whole orange* out of the box.

Mum grabs my arm before I can slice the orange in two. 'Wait, I didn't order any of this. We'll have to trigger a return request.'

'It's fine, Mum. Trust me.' I slice the orange in half, take her hand and guide her to her armchair. 'Now, sit and eat.'

For some reason I can't get enough of the confusion on her face as I balance a plate on her knees. She just stares at the orange half in front of her. I can see her calculating how many weeks of hunger we face if we're charged for it.

'Enjoy.' I leave her sitting there and get back to stirring the mushrooms. The veg sausages seem dry but they smell delicious.

Mum's only eaten a quarter of her orange when I turn back, so I carry our two plates over and sit next to her.

'You can eat all of that, you know.' I settle in and take a bite of sausage.

Mum watches me for a while and then her eyes track down to the pile on her plate. Finally, she turns to me again. 'What's going on?'

A grin with full cheeks. 'Told you I'd handle it.' The sausage is sort of disgusting and sort of delicious at the same time.

Mum watches me eat, her mouth a straight line. 'Coutlyn, what have you done?'

Fork on the plate, I click the comscreen on and bring up my deets. My name. My address. My ration points. At least the glitch doesn't seem to be affecting the stuff I added.

Mum blinks, still taking it in, then motions with her hand to bring up her own deets. They're all still there. She turns to me and at last I see a flicker of delight cross her eyes.

'I know, right?' I raise my eyebrows at the amazingness of it all and finally Mum lets out a disbelieving laugh. It's the best sound in the universe.

'But ... *how*?' she asks, shaking her head.

'Well ...' I cringe. 'It's probably best if you don't know, but from now on you'll have your own rations all to yourself. Pretty good, huh?'

Mum's smile threatens to fade. I can see her fighting to hold it in place. 'Scout, tell me how this happened.'

I have no idea how to say this. I've been shuffling through various versions in my mind – everything between an outright lie and simply refusing to say anything – but I realise now that I can't lie about this, not to Mum.

Carefully I take her through last night, trying to make it clear that I didn't plan any of it. Mum's quiet as I talk, listening rather than reacting. There might have been a time when death freaked people out; I've studied the same history course as chipped kids who go to school. But these days we see death all the time. On the news, for a start, but also when retirees on 300 ration points a day waste away, or when unchipped refugees can't access water.

Mum asks some questions about the woman. I say nothing about the weird stuff on her history map. Mum nods faintly once or twice but otherwise stares at the floorboards as she takes it all in. So then I move straight into the deets I've already added online. How no-one, not even government officials, could tell that the chip wasn't on my wrist since I was born.

It's only when I tell Mum that I've registered for the select-entry test that she snaps back into focus. 'Wait. You've registered already?'

'Yeah. So? I thought that's what you wanted.'

She doesn't reply, just leaves the plate on the arm of the chair, stands and takes a few steps towards the comscreen; it's black now, on standby, but still somehow imposing because of its size. Her outline is reflected in the screen but I can't make out her expression.

After a while, I lean forward. 'Are you … angry?'

'No, Scout.' She turns back to me and forces a smile. 'I'm … sorry for that woman but I've brought you too far down this path to be angry about what you did.' She shakes her head. 'I only wish you'd discussed this with me before you registered for the test. It would have been much safer if you'd registered with *my* chip. I could have accessed that woman's rations and you could have just …'

She trails off but I know what she was going to say. I could have just stepped into her life. I could have taken over her chip. But it's such a non-solution; we'd just be transferring all my problems to her. I can't believe we're still discussing this. My eyes drop to the mushrooms and sausage on her plate; she hasn't even touched them.

'You need to discuss these things with me first, okay? This room is registered to *me*.'

'So?'

Mum lets out a sigh, but instead of answering she turns away, carrying her plate to the sink and standing to bite at the sausage with her back to me. Her hands shake slightly as she eats; she must have been hungrier than she was letting on.

After a while she turns to me and leans backwards against the sink. 'You're a smart kid, Scout,' she says. And then, almost to herself, 'You'll have to be.'

I stand and move towards her, trying to read her expression. 'I did it, Mum. Didn't I tell you that I'd handle it?'

'Yes, Scout. You did.' The air about her is more hope than happiness, but I reach in for a hug anyway.

'It's going to be okay now,' I say, my head tucked under her chin. Mum doesn't say anything but I feel her arms hold me tighter.

Silently, I make a pact.

From now on, it's my turn to give back to Mum. For all that she's done for me, all that she's given up, I'm going to pay her back.

CHAPTER THREE

A MESSAGE IS WAITING from Alistair when I wake up the next morning: *Don't know how you did it, but pleased nonetheless. Try some practice tests if you're feeling nervous. Once again, Agent X, you surprise me.* ⊗

The emotiphone at the end is set to trigger cheers and applause as soon as it registers my eye-focus. So utterly corny that I groan and make a face, laughing at the screen.

It's a while since he's used that nickname, Agent X. A top code-cracker, in hiding from the government. That was me for as long as I can remember.

I must have been six years old, home alone while Mum was at work, when I worked out how to unlock our door. Those long hours in our room used to feel like a lifetime each day. I was already at the front gate when Alistair found me.

I remember Mum and Alistair talking that evening, but I don't remember what they said. All I know is that soon after,

Alistair started sending me little onscreen games. Each day, he'd send me a new code to crack. At least, that's how he described it. But as it turns out, he was taking me step-by-step through programming basics.

I send an emotiphone back to Alistair – a cheering emoji with a posh voice saying 'thank-you, thank-you, thank-you' and applause in the background. Then I spend some time on the practice tests he linked to. I only have to revise one of the maths questions and grit my teeth through a reading comprehension. But soon my mind turns to the world outside that door – and my list of all the wonderful things I can do, the same as all other citizens.

I'm nearly at the overpass to Footscray Station when my steps slow and I find myself glancing up at the security cameras.

When I was little, Mum refused to bring me past this part of town. That was before I understood. I still remember the tightness in my chest as I begged her, holding back the tears, promising extra chores and trying to tempt her with my share of her rations. *Please, Mum. Please. Please.*

I would have done anything to ride on the fast train. Just once. Just to see.

My heart lifts as I step into the crowd, allowing them to pull me along, through security and then through the barrier gate, a train line stretching like a red carpet before me. A ticket to the entire city.

I leap onto the carriage like a kid, then force myself to slow down and act natural. My senses are on overload. So many bodies packed in tight. The smell of new plastic and the taste of rubber. For some reason the bored expressions everywhere make my grin grow even bigger. A couple of guys in Murdoch High School uniforms seem to have noticed my good mood, so I manoeuvre my way to a window, stumbling as the hovering carriage slides into motion and then bracing a shoulder against the window. My forehead presses against the thick glass as I watch the world blur, feeling the speed through every part of my body.

We reach Central Station in no time at all, and I step off with what I hope is the same lazy expression as everyone else.

Across the road from Central Station, I take the steps two at a time up to the State Library. This is all so easy. Usually it takes fifty minutes by bike to make it here.

You could pretty much call this place my second home, I've spent so much time in here, partly because you don't need a chip to get inside. The security system is all about keeping print books in, rather than keeping anyone out.

I could use my compad to read, of course. Going to the library is more about the people coming and going. Normal people. The nation's citizens. When I'm here, I can belong.

The terminal in the furthest corner is free so I settle in, glad to be away from passing traffic. I actually have the compad out of my pocket before I realise I don't have to hack in to trigger the start of a session. There aren't many people around. A skinny old man is working a few terminals down but I can't see anyone else, so I pull the slip of paper out of my pocket, carefully folded around the chip. Holding it between finger and palm, I swipe the sensor.

Access granted. I'll never grow tired of that ping.

At first I just flick through the news, but that gets sort of depressing so I decide to check out the entrance scores for uni courses and end up exactly where I always do: Bachelor of Bioengineering. I know that it's possible to feed way more people than they do now, even with the same amount of water. I've read heaps about it, and I have the best incentive of anyone to help make it happen. The cut-off score at Monash Uni is 87, and 83 at La Trobe. Not sure if I'll get that kind of score, but getting into the right high school will be a good start.

I'm adding up the course fees when I hear voices murmuring behind me, and turn to see two guys in Murdoch High School uniforms leaning against the back wall. One of them is bulky and the other lean. They kind of look like the guys I saw on the train, but that would be weird.

The slimmer guy was watching as I glanced his way, so I turn back to the terminal and keep reading.

Or I try to, anyway. But I end up reading the same sentence three times over because I can't get my mind off the guys at the back wall. They're standing at the only spot in the library that has a direct sightline to my screen.

After a while I can't stand it anymore and swivel in my seat, squinting along the row of terminals as if I'm on the lookout for someone I know.

They're still there, whispering to each other. When they see me looking around they go still, the bigger one standing away from the wall like he's getting ready to come over.

I spin back to the screen, trying to work out what's going on. Maybe I'm being paranoid, but what if I'm not?

Why would they be following me?

Automatically my hand moves to the slip of paper in my pocket. It feels hot against my hip. I can't help wondering if I'll ever wish I could undo what happened that night in the cave.

The comscreen churns into logoff as I grab my gear. I head the long way round the rows of terminals and through the kids' corner.

At a side exit, I slip outside. The sensors go *tuk* as I leave, quiet reminders that I'm not off-grid anymore.

I blend with the crowd as best as I can and, after half a block, I turn down Little Lonsdale Street and then quickly again into a side alley so I can't be seen from Swanston Boulevard.

Leaning backwards against the wall, I check for an escape route if I need it, glad to see that the alley leads to another street at the end. There's a shoe shop down here, and a row of padlocked rubbish skips, but little else.

Accessing the grid on a compad is a complete pain because the screen's so small. You end up scrolling and enlarging a lot. And getting lost. But I'm used to it by now. I already have a smokescreen set up, so I trigger that and hack straight into the grid.

Moving fast, I scroll across to find the library, and then

terminal fifteen. There's a bright dot at number fourteen now, but no dots at the back wall.

My lips feel dry and I lick them against the cool air, tracking backwards in time to three minutes ago, four, five …

Until I find them. Two dots, at the back wall: the guys in Murdoch High School uniforms.

I tag them both with '???' to make sure I can find them again, and then follow their movements since I slipped away from the library.

They left only seconds after I did, out the front entrance and then along Swanston Boulevard, the same direction as me.

Now that I've tagged them it's easy to track them in real time, so I skip forwards to access the grid at the present moment.

The world goes still around me. Right now, they're standing at the same corner I turned down only a few minutes ago. *It could still be a coincidence,* I tell myself, but it's more a desperate plea than anything else.

All I can do is shake my head as I watch the two dots move down Little Lonsdale Street towards my alleyway. Somehow, those two guys must have access to the grid, and they're using it to track my chip.

Every nerve in my body is telling me to run for it, but what would be the point? As long as I still hold the chip, they'll be able to trace me.

There's no time to plan, so I slip between two of the rubbish skips. Pointless, since they'll be able to find me here, but I can't just stand in the open.

Staying as quiet as I can, I track the two dots as they turn down the alleyway, moving ever closer to mine on the grid. They're a few metres from my hiding place when I catch some hushed words.

'... careful not to scare ...'

'... hasn't jumped already.'

A breath, and I step out from behind the skip. 'Stay where you are!' My arm points right at them, straight as an arrow.

Both guys jolt to a stop at the tone of my voice. The bigger of the two places his hands on his hips and nods. He's broad, dark-skinned and so sure of himself that he seems anchored to the earth.

I'm surprised that it's the thin one who goes to talk first, but when he steps towards me I step back and yell, 'Don't come any closer!'

Head bowed, he raises both hands. 'Okay, okay. We're just ... pleased to meet you.'

I'm momentarily speechless at such an odd thing to say. I cross my arms, still ready to bolt if I need to.

The slender guy glances at the other, and then back to me. 'Can we go somewhere to talk?'

'Here's fine.'

He lifts his hands higher, urging me to stay calm. 'Okay, just don't disappear on us.'

I make this face that's meant to say *don't tell me what to do*, even though there's no way to disappear when they're obviously tracking me on the grid. That's my whole problem.

'Okay.' His hands clasp beneath his chin, his thin face shadowed by straight dark hair. 'I'm Mason Cohen, and this is Boc … Charles Bocworth.' A pause, but I don't react. 'We've seen what you can do. Not in person … but on the grid. We just want to talk to you about it. We're not going to give you away.'

Boc drops his hands from his hips. 'We want to learn how you do it.'

They're both watching me closely, two camera lenses recording my every expression; it's the strangest feeling. Two guys in elite-school uniforms, who have clearly spent their whole lives on top-level rations, want to talk to *me*.

Though, of course, it's not really me they want to talk to, I remind myself. I can't help wondering what they would make of the woman if they were speaking to her instead of me.

I push my chin forwards. 'How did you track me? You're not with the police?'

Again, they glance at each other. Mason pulls out his compad, holding it out so I can see. 'I'll show you?'

Arms still crossed, I shuffle forwards barely enough to be able to see his screen. A couple wanders past with their arms linked, so we all go quiet until they pass.

'Here.' Mason taps the screen and immediately the grid appears. No smokescreen, I notice. 'See this? It's a map of us right here, right now. This is how the government tracks crims and checks illegal suspects, yeah?'

'Okay.' *Don't give anything away.*

His fingers move fast, so skilled at playing the grid that I find myself watching them rather than the screen. 'It's sort of a hobby of ours, dropping in and watching stuff,' Mason continues. 'That's how we noticed your gaps.'

It's only now that I focus on the screen and have to suck in a breath at the location: my cave at Footscray Park.

The air goes dry in my throat as he brings up the history map and types in a date and time: six o'clock, two nights ago. The same moment when that woman seemed to just *appear* out of nowhere.

'We've been waiting for you to come back,' Boc says simply.

I search for words that won't give me away, trying to get my head around all this. 'But how did you know where I'd be when I ... came back?' I ask slowly.

'We found the dead end. On the grid, I mean.' Immediately Mason keys a new date into the history grid, nearly two years ago. And there it is, the dot in the exact same spot in my cave. 'We know that you have to return to the same location, so we've been watching.'

'This is the first time we've had real proof that it's possible,' finishes Boc.

They're both staring at me, two sets of eyes tracking my every change of expression. It's the most unnerving feeling. I'm not used to being around people this close to my age, but even I can see this is weird.

'Sorry, I have to ask. When were you born?' Mason asks quietly.

'It's all on the grid,' I say slowly. '24th of March, 2070.'

'No, he means ... really,' Boc steps in. 'When were you *really* born?'

'I don't know,' I say, because they're not asking about me. They're asking when that woman was born. This is all about her. 'Around 2024,' I say dryly, estimating that the woman looked around sixty years old. Dumb joke, but they're not making any sense either.

Mason's whole face breaks into a broad smile. He leans so close that for a moment I think he's going to breathe me in. 'It's so, so good to *finally* meet you,' he says, his voice low. 'We can help you too, if you need. We have a place where you can stay—'

'Listen,' I say, backing away. 'I'm sorry, but you've made a mistake. It's just a glitch in the chip. It's not what you think.' Whatever that is.

'Wait, please.' Mason holds out his hands. 'We're not going to expose you. We just want to ask —'

'I can't help you, okay?' I snap over the top of him. 'It's a fault in the system, that's all. Maybe there was something blocking the signal.'

'— but I need your help to understand where I'm going wrong.' Mason's voice is pleading and breathless. Boc goes to move forward, but stops himself and balls his fists.

'Leave me alone!' I spin away and sprint down the alley.

When I turn at the end, I'm glad that they haven't tried to follow.

The train trip home is different from the trip in. I stand with my back to the corner of the carriage, watching people swaying around me. Somehow, I've lost the fun of the moment.

What were those guys talking about? In my head I go over the conversation, trying to make sense of it. They weren't police, at least, or government officials. But still.

As soon as I get home, I fire up the comscreen to check for myself, make sure what Mason showed me was real.

Quickly, I set up the smokescreen and head straight to the woman's history map from nearly two years ago. There she is, in my cave. The seconds tick past ...

She disappears.

What's going on? I wet my lips and begin to track backwards, watching her dot appear again and then following her movements in reverse before she came to Footscray Park two years ago. She'd walked there in the early hours of the morning from the city tip. Food scraps maybe? There's not much food waste these days; I know from experience that there's little reward from scavenging in the tip.

I sit back, thinking, then lean forwards again.

I've tagged Mason and Boc, so I find their dots and track them back to the same date as when the woman was at the tip. They're together, at basement level somewhere in Moonee Ponds. No surprise. It's a rich person's suburb, where families still live in entire houses all to themselves. In my mind, I picture them hunched over a comscreen, tracking the exact same history map that I was just watching.

Now I return to study that woman's history map, tracking backwards again. Two days earlier, the worm hits another gap.

I lean back in the chair, trying to make sense of what I'm seeing. It could be a complete fabrication, of course. Anyone with enough coding skill could add glitchy stuff like that to the grid. But those guys said they'd hacked into the grid, not that they'd been messing with it.

We've been waiting for you to come back.

We know you have to return to the same location.

Leaning forwards again, I zoom the history map right out so that I can see years at a time. The mistake I made last time was not tracking her worm over enough years. Now I move backwards in larger chunks of time: one year, two, five …

After a gap of seventeen years, I find her again. In the same spot at the tip is another moment when the woman's dot disappears. In 2065 she spent three hours at the tip, but after that the worm comes to a dead end again. It makes no sense.

When I zoom out as far as I can, I see that her map goes back as far as 2050, but that's the year chips first started being inserted, so it's not clear when she was born. She looked way older than that.

Only now does a thought come to me. I pull up the map from six o'clock the night I stormed out on Mum, then change my mind and switch to ten o'clock the same night.

I can't find the exact moment when I first found that woman, but I know more or less what time I walked out on Mum. So I use that to make a rough guess of when I found the woman lying under my blanket.

Instead of zooming out, looking at the history map over a number of years, I zoom right in, tracking her worm minute by minute, second by second. Nothing stands out, so I zoom in closer still and track her history map millisecond by millisecond.

It's slow going and I give up more than once, rubbing my eyes and standing up to stretch before coming back. I'm not even sure what I'm expecting to prove, but when I find the moment I've been searching for I just sit here and stare at the screen.

At 10.17 and 09.34 seconds, on the night I found that woman, is a gap in her history map.

It only lasted a couple of milliseconds but that was the moment that made me stop and turn back, when her frame flickered in front of me as if she were a hologram. Matching that same moment on the woman's history map is a gap of 0.026 seconds.

Whatever was going on with this woman, I saw it happen.

CHAPTER FOUR

FOR MOST OF the night I lie with my eyes closed, replaying the night I found that woman. The way her frame flickered in front of me ...

At the time I thought I'd lost concentration for a moment, blinked, perhaps, but now I realise that I saw something very weird. Something impossible.

When Mum's alarm sounds I'm immediately awake, but I lie still and listen to the faint rustle of fabric as she dresses and leaves. As soon as the front door engages, I'm up and clicking the comscreen on.

It takes me three minutes to hack into the computer in Mason's basement. Maybe I'll be able to uncover a clue that will help me work out what's going on.

There's a heap of noise to get past – internet searches, news updates, messages between friends and family. I don't know what I'm trying to find, exactly, so it's hard knowing what to search for.

I skim through some day-to-day messages and filter out basics like ration points, then I search for 'gap' or even 'history map'. Nothing interesting comes up. I try a few more key words, and then type in certain dates and grid references. No luck.

I think for a bit, and come up blank.

So then I just go browsing, trying to find clues in their daily lives. It feels somehow wrong trawling through their private stuff, but the slight guilt isn't enough to make me stop. Whatever's going on, whatever that woman was doing, I need to find out what it was. From watching how well Mason knew his way around the grid, I can tell that he knows how to hack other stuff too.

A lot of the time I just sift through boring stuff in case it uncovers some sort of clue. Mason's school reports are littered with national academic awards. The guy clearly has a seriously high mega-IQ.

Boc's reports are okay, but I can tell that school isn't exactly a priority. Most weekends it looks like he heads out of the city to go mountain biking. I spend ages squinting at the screen to make sure I'm reading the map contours right because when he's coming down the side of a mountain, the terrain he covers is insane.

When he isn't flying down a mountainside, Boc trains with a climbing group that calls itself 'The Spiderboys' because they scale city buildings rather than heading out to cliff faces. He was even arrested once, but from the way it was written up in the news, it seemed like a slap on the wrist more than anything else.

The headline is: FUTURE ELITES AIM FOR THE SKY. There's a picture of Boc next to some guy with pale skin and black hair called Amon Lang. I roll my eyes. If anyone on F-level rations had been caught climbing the Macquarie Bank building, they'd have been hit with a permanent crim stamp.

Just from pulling up their history maps over the past six months, I actually get a pretty clear idea of who these guys are. Mason's map is neat and contained, travelling the same path to school and back, with most of his spare time spent in his basement. Boc's looks like a crazy scribble flower, looping all over the city and spiking out to mountain areas every few weeks. He's always seeing people, always doing stuff.

As my eyes travel over Boc's crazy scribble, though, I realise there's a constant, in the centre of his flower. Mason. Every few days, Boc always returns to his centre.

———————————

The next morning, I'm searching through Boc's computer when I find a document – a letter from Boc addressed to the school principal. It's an apology after Boc was suspended for triggering lockdown in the middle of exam week. In it, he says he's sorry for the trouble he caused but then goes on to say that the school should be aware how easy it is to hack its security, as if he did them a favour.

Sort of interesting, but it still has nothing to do with gaps in anyone's history map.

I'm sifting through messages between Mason and Boc from around that time, when I realise that the identity tags are out of sequence. My eyes narrow at that. Interesting. Some of the messages must have been swiped from both hard drives.

It takes me a while to hack into the mainframe backups and then it takes me a day to work out how to bring up Mason and Boc's messages out of all the billions stored in there. Not easy when a mega brain like Mason was trying to hide them.

After some clever workarounds and by targeting specific dates, I manage to find the exchange that Mason was trying to hide.

Once I start reading, it all makes sense. It seems that Mason was the one who hacked into school security and wanted to own up for what he did. It took Boc two days to talk Mason out of it. It was Boc's idea, so he thought he should be the one to take the hit. I guess they'd stopped talking face to face because the arguing all happens via messaging, even during school hours.

It makes me a bit less wary about these guys, somehow; they just get up to a bit of hacking and stuff. At the same time, I can't help being disappointed. None of it had anything to do with people disappearing after all.

———————————

By the end of the day I'm still no closer to working out what's going on, so I move on to a different search tactic. How do you find something when you're not sure what you're searching for?

Just go looking for the stuff that people are trying to hide.

I've already worked out how to access emails that were deleted, so the next day I write a bot that filters through all the deleted files that still exist on the mainframe backup, searching for anything that originated from Mason's or Boc's computers.

The comscreen starts churning through. For a while I sit and watch, then I leave it chugging and cook some oats for breakfast.

When I come back it's still searching, but already some files have begun to appear: a whole new series of emails between Mason and Boc and months of browsing history. All stuff they tried to delete.

No-one's watching, but I make a show of breathing on my fingernails and polishing them on my pyjama top. One of the best things about hacking is the buzz you get when you find your way into some place you're not meant to be.

I can tell that I'm onto something as soon as I start reading.

It's possible, I promise it is, Mason writes in the earliest message on the list. *Not in some future reality, once a time machine's been invented. Time travel is possible and always has been. It all makes sense once you understand the true nature of time.*

I read that email through three times, mouthing the words to make sure that I'm reading right. This is crazy. I can't keep reading fast enough.

Most of the deleted browsing history is linked to sites about something called Relative Time Theory and a lot of the emails are from Mason explaining it to Boc.

I get the feeling that they were talking during the day and then messaging at night. Some emails seem to pick up in the middle of a conversation and then drop out before it's finished,

I guess when they met up again at school. But even with the gaps, I find myself reading through the strangest, most amazing of ideas …

All our lives, we've been moving with the flow of time because that's all we know, that's what we expect, says Mason in one email. *But in truth, time isn't flowing. Reality only exists as separate moments, like frames in a movie.*

Or dots in the grid? from Boc.

Mason again: *Yes, that's it exactly. We think we move with the flow of time, allowing it to carry us along because that's what we believe is happening. Our mistake is that we believe time is outside ourselves. Steady. It's not. The way we connect with time is changeable. That's the clue.*

That's the clue …

Except, I can't find the rest of that message sequence. I search around for a while, and read through one of the sites on Relative Time Theory until my brain is about to explode.

After that, I give up on the site and pick up another conversation:

We already experience changes in time without realising, Mason writes. *Sometimes whole hours, whole days, fly past. Right? Other times, when you face a split-second crisis, everything slows down. Your mind will slow its experience of time in order to survive. Think about it. Our sense of time changes because we control the passage of time within ourselves.*

I lean back, thinking it through. I've never heard time described this way. *We control the passage of time within ourselves.*

Soon I lean forwards and re-trigger the session. I pick up the rest of the conversation:

That's all very well about controlling time, Einstein, Boc says in another message. *But you haven't said anything about travelling through time. Jumping ahead like the gap you found on the grid. That's way different.*

Mason replies: *I had trouble getting my get my head around that, too. Maybe it will help if you think of time as a river. Okay with that?*

Sure. Okay. The river of time.

Mason continues. *Everyone thinks they're stuck inside the present moment, being carried along with the flow of time. But the whole river exists at once, not just the bit you're travelling in, right?*

Got it.

So instead of being swept along with the river, imagine if you could freeze it. Then you could move to a different part of the river — just pick whichever part of time you want to be — then unfreeze the river so time starts flowing again. Only you've changed where you are in it.

Yeah, I guess. Except time isn't really a river is it, Mase?

No, Boc — I was making a point. Here's the thing you need to understand: we need to learn how to slow our sense of time to a stop. From there, you have the power to return at any point you choose. In theory, at least.

Fine. No problem, replies Boc. *But how exactly do you plan to do that?*

Mason's reply came back as a single word: *Meditation.*

———————

Alistair's in the share kitchen when I collect our evening delivery on Saturday. 'Agent X, reporting for duty?' he calls slowly with his eyes still on the chopping board.

I dump our bag on the island bench and check out his spread of ingredients. Baby carrots, bean shoots and a shrivelled green capsicum half. 'What you cooking?'

'Stir-fry surprise.'

'What's the surprise?'

'Leftover chilli beans,' he says, and glances up. 'We're in beta testing. Want some?'

I shake my head, chin in my hands, because of course it's rude to accept someone else's rations, even a five-year-old kid knows that. But I keep watching anyway. Now that we have enough rations to cook some decent meals, I'm on the lookout for ideas.

We're quiet while he chops, but that's just how it is if you want to catch up with Alistair. It's a slower world where he lives, one with few words.

'How long until the test?' Alistair says after a while, still looking at the chopping board.

'Four days.'

'How'd the practice tests go?'

'They were okay. I got 93 for maths and 89 for problem solving.'

'Reading comprehension?' He picks up the half capsicum and slowly begins to scrape out the seeds. His hands look stiff as he works, as if his joints need to be oiled.

When I just shrug, he stops scraping and waits.

A sigh. '76?'

'That's okay. It's enough.' Alistair pushes his chin forwards when he sees the look on my face. 'You'll be fine, Scout.'

'Maybe.' But I don't say more than that. Don't want to jinx it by hoping too hard.

Mum's probably wondering why I'm taking so long, but I don't take our delivery back yet. Instead I hang around, pulling dry skin from beside a fingernail.

'Have you heard of something called Relative Time Theory?' I ask.

Alistair stops with the capsicum and looks up. 'Can't say that I have.'

'It's sort of the idea that time is just in our mind. That it comes from the way our brains make sense of each separate moment.'

There's no movement from Alistair at first, he just stares at a point on the bench.

I've almost given up on a reply when he says, 'Time definitely seems different for me these days. Each year seems to fly past faster than the last.' A slow shrug brings him out of his thoughts as he focuses on me. 'Who knows? Maybe you're onto something.'

I think about showing him the gap in that woman's history map, but if I head down that path, I'd have to tell him where the chip came from.

Years ago, Mum sat me down and told me how dangerous it could be for the people we care about if I was ever found out as illegal. There's no way I want to put Alistair in danger, so we've always had a bit of a speak-no-evil, hear-no-evil agreement between us.

I'm not sure where to go next, but I don't want to stop. 'Some people believe that if we understand time properly –' I search for the right words. 'We can learn how to move wherever we want in it.'

A frown. 'Where did this come from?'

'Just something I read.'

Alistair goes quiet again. 'So you're saying we could travel through time if we understood it properly? A case of mind over matter?'

'Sort of. I guess …'

'Interesting,' he says. 'Never heard of that one before.'

'Yeah, don't worry.' Now that I'm saying it out loud, it sounds impossible. 'I know it sounds crazy.'

'Maybe it does.' Alistair's watching me closely. 'But they said the same about lots of things that turned out to be true. Ever heard of Galileo?'

'Yeah. Think so.'

'I'll send you a link.'

'Okay, thanks Alistair. Better go.' I grab our delivery and head for the hall. 'Hope the beta testing is a success.'

———————

Studying takes over the next few days. It's easier to concentrate now that I'm on full rations, but I also find out how tired you get when you eat a full lunch. I decide to keep hungry enough to stay alert. Calm but focused, that's the goal.

Every now and then, I drop in on Mason and Boc during a study break. I'm sure they're watching me too. The way I see it, I'm simply returning the favour. Once I even catch them in the middle of an argument, Mason saying that it's worth a try and Boc telling him it's a waste of time. I'm not sure what the 'it' is, though.

I even have a go at meditating once, sitting on the end of the bed, concentrating on my breathing and allowing my mind to sink. It gives the sensation of tension trickling from my brain and into the base of my neck. It's really refreshing, and I'm better able to concentrate after I finish.

Do I reach the point where time seems to slow?

No way. Not even close.

On the day of the test, Mum arranges to start work late and catches a train in with me. It's not just for moral support. She hasn't said it out loud, but I know she wants to be there just in case. I've double-checked the deets on the chip and we've talked through it all, but this is the first time it's being tested for real.

We come out of the concourse at Southern Station, and it's as if the city is being overtaken by thirteen- and fourteen-year-olds, moving in bunches of three or four, or sticking close to their parents. Everyone applying for a select-entry school has to sit this test; twenty-two schools in total now that Karoly High School opened last year. Pretty much everyone who thinks they have a chance is currently making their way to the Exhibition Building.

There was a time when these select-entry schools were only for the kids who couldn't afford the traditional elites, but these days everyone's desperate to get in. The game isn't so much about who you know; it's all about your contribution to the state. Or, in the case of everyone my age, it's about how much you're likely to contribute in the future. Your IP: intelligence potential.

Everything started changing around the time the ration system was brought in. And then when Christophe Eichmann won the Nobel Prize in physics, Mum says there was a huge jump in kids applying. He went to Nossal High, one of the first select-entry schools, and is the guy who invented the thermal inverter, which harnesses the hot winds that are whipped up during a heatwave and uses them to mega-load solar energy.

Everyone has to learn about Christophe Eichmann because he's the goal we're all aiming for, basically. His ration level would have been so high that no letter exists to describe it. He died in 2065 but I'm sure the entire country sends him a prayer of thanks on days when the world is a fan-forced oven and we get to flick on the air-con.

We make it to the entrance foyer with about a zillion other applicants and shuffle obediently towards the security gate. Most of the parents are already saying their goodbyes, but Mum stays close. We near the centre gate and I can see the photo IDs flashing up on a comscreen to one side as each person walks through.

Mum squeezes my forearm as my turn comes, then hangs back as I wipe my palms against my thighs and walk through the gate. My photo comes up, just like it has for everyone else. In it, I'm wearing a white shirt with a school emblem half chopped off at the bottom. Photoshopped in, of course.

The woman sitting at the entrance desk doesn't even glance up and I find myself walking free, no longer crammed in with the crowd. I turn to look back at Mum, standing to one side on the other side of the gate, and almost cause a jam in the flow because I think I see tears in her eyes.

She raises her eyebrows. *Keep going.*

Still I hesitate, but by now she's laughing as she shakes her head. *Keep going already.* I can't help grinning as I wave at Mum one more time. No-one else would understand the mountain we just climbed. Of any test I'm doing today, the entrance gate was by far the largest.

With all the others, I head into the massive halls. So many desks laid out row after row, so many others aiming for the same goal. I don't let the nerves spike. At least for once, I'm on equal footing. For the first time in my life, I have just as much chance as anyone else.

CHAPTER FIVE

IT TAKES FIVE days before I receive an automated email from the selection co-ordinator: 'Congratulations on successfully completing phase one of your application to attend Karoly High School in 2085. Please book an interview for phase two by following the instructions here.'

My heart lifts to the ceiling before slapping to the floor as I read on. The email also requests the contact details of a registered teacher who is willing to give a verbal reference.

Straight away, I hit Mum's work number. 'They want to speak to one of my teachers,' I blurt as soon as she answers. 'What are we going to do?'

A pause. 'Scout, I'm with a client right now.' Considering she's at work, I should have expected that. 'But I'll ... wait. You made it through?'

It gets a bit fun from there because the client who's with

Mum has a son who just finished year twelve at Nossal, so she joins in with the celebration.

Mum's about to hang up, when she says, 'And Coutlyn. We'll talk later, okay?'

'Yeah. Thanks, Mum.'

As the compad goes dim I breathe out and let my shoulders drop. I just did exactly what I'd promised myself I wouldn't: asked Mum to solve a problem when I should be doing that myself. Maybe I can set up an automated voice recording, I don't know. I have two weeks to work it out.

Mum's so pleased about me getting an interview that we head into the city for dinner. She does her hair up in this fancy French roll and lets me borrow a work shirt and pants, which is the best we can manage in terms of dressing up.

The restaurant is amazing – Oceanic Fusion – but I can't help noticing some of the other diners in here with us. Tight-cropped hair, cool linen slacks and fitted shirts. It's not that Mum looks old compared to the other women in here, but she does look old-fashioned.

I'm already saving credits, so I add another line to my pact. Mum's next birthday is a couple of months away and it's going to make up for all the others.

We're on the fast train, nearly at Footscray Station when Mum smiles over at me, rocking with the movement of the carriage. 'Remember when you were six?'

'Yeah. I remember. Made your life easy, didn't I?'

She laughs. 'You've come a long way since then.'

We shuffle through security then walk freer as the crowd spreads. Outside the station we've almost reached the crossing point when two figures walk up to us. They're both in Murdoch High School uniforms. Mason and Boc.

They were looking at me, but something about the way Mum and I stop at the same time must make it obvious that we're together, and it's the strangest thing because for a moment it's as if everything stalls and we're all gaping at each other in slow motion. Each millisecond feels like a hundred as I try to work out what to do.

Mum takes my hand and goes to walk around them, just as Mason recovers and says: 'Hey. I was hoping to catch you.'

Mum stops and looks at me quizzically.

I try not to cringe. 'Um … this is Mason. And Charles. We met at the State Library. And they ah … gave me some tips about the select-entry test.' A lie wrapped in the truth.

Mum's expression shifts from wary to curious as her eyes travel over their uniforms. I'm acting as if this is no big deal. But inside, my heart is racing. What are they going to ask?

'Pleased to meet you.' Boc steps forward and offers a hand, tipping his head as he shakes. 'We don't mean to intrude.'

'No, that's, ah … fine.' Mum glances my way before turning back to Boc. Now it's his hair that catches her attention, short and freshly cut. 'It's nice to meet you.'

'Likewise.' Now Mason holds out a hand.

I should be annoyed with them for catching me out like this, following me still, but they're both so polite, so clean-cut, that I actually get this weird sort of lift inside at being able to introduce them. As if knowing people like this makes me a better citizen, or something.

'Call me Miya,' Mum says, and finally finds a smile.

'Listen, this isn't a good time,' I say as clearly as I can. *Not in front of Mum.*

'It's all right. I'll leave you to chat.' Mum as good as beams at Mason and Boc before turning to raise her eyes meaningfully at me. 'I'll check out some window displays while I'm waiting.'

'Won't be long,' I tell Mum.

We're all quiet while she crosses the street and wanders over to a clothing display window.

At least I know what they're up to this time. Sort of. I lift my chin. 'You have to stop following me.'

'Sorry.' Mason glances at Mum again. 'You were on the train when I checked the grid, I didn't realise you were with someone.'

'Has that woman given you a place to stay?' Boc jerks his head backwards over a shoulder. They would have seen Mum's dot when they were watching me at home. 'Who is she?'

I obviously can't say that she's my mum. It wouldn't add up. The woman from the cave was time skipping when Mum was a kid. 'Just a friend.'

'Does she know how to jump?'

'No.'

Mason makes a *duh* face at Boc and then sort of apologises at me, as if he's sure we're thinking the same thing. They would have seen gaps on her history map if she knew how to jump.

To be safe, I add: 'She's just giving me a place to stay, that's all.'

Mason glances across the street at Mum then back at me. 'Listen. I'm sorry. It's just, I'm having trouble and I thought you might be able to help –'

It's the strangest feeling, having something that they want. Power, or knowledge or whatever it is. Not that I actually have it.

I shake my head. 'I don't think I can –'

'Just answer a couple of questions, that's all I ask.'

Still shaking. 'I'm sorry. I can't.'

Mum finishes with the clothing shop and moves to the next one along, just as Mason steps forwards. But having her here forces me to face up to how exposed we are. If Mason and Boc work out I'm not that woman, they'll work out I stole the chip. If I'm caught, it means jail for Mum too.

I take a step back the same distance that Mason just stepped forward, shaking my head. 'I'm sorry, I can't help you.' I dash past them and head straight for Mum.

I doze through the night, never fully finding sleep, but not exactly awake either. After a bathroom trip around dawn I try to meditate lying on my back in bed, but it's hard doing that with so many questions running through my mind. What was going on with that woman? What do Mason and Boc want to learn – how to travel through time?

An idea comes to me as I open my eyes. Glancing over at

Mum's sleeping form, I get up carefully to avoid waking her. Then I slide the chip between the base of the armchair and its cushion. Anyone who happens to hack into the grid will think I'm sitting here and watching the news. Not thinking about anyone or anything in particular.

I leave a note for Mum and then make my way outside, along our street and towards Footscray Park. I wasn't expecting how this would feel, back to the me that I've always known. It's as if I can breathe again now that I'm off-grid, and I can't help imagining Mason or Boc watching my dot, thinking they have me tagged at home when I'm not.

Just like so many other times before, I check for other people around and pick an early-morning jogger making his way towards me, increasing my pace to make sure I reach Ballarat Road at the same time he does. I have the compad with me, but I won't need to use it. He jogs on the spot impatiently as we wait for the ping. As soon as the smartcars come to a stop, he sprints across the road and through the entrance to the park before disappearing down the path.

I follow at my own pace.

The whole park is on the side of a hill, sloping down to the canal. Early morning light rims the shapes and shadows. It's thick with so many shrubs and trees that you can't see from one winding path to another. They're mostly natives these days, but a couple of big old oaks and even an elm have managed to survive the drought.

When I near the ghost gum that covers the entrance to the

cave, I check out my usual danger points – places that I've worked out offer someone even a slim chance of catching a glimpse of me here. I've learnt to take my time, play it safe.

As soon as I'm sure that no-one can see, I tiptoe across the garden bed, keeping my hands lifted above the native grasses to avoid their stinging paper cuts. I've only gone a few paces when I stop, crouching low and hanging back from the entrance. I don't want to go any further.

She's still there.

At least, her remains are. My eyes travel cautiously over the long, narrow lumps of her legs beneath the blanket as cool air drifts from within the cave. The scene is so still, so terribly quiet. The loneliness of this place settles around me once more.

Why did I come? To check if she was still here, I guess.

Still crouching, I rest my chin on a knee. The blanket is threadbare with patches of mould and other stuff I don't want to go near. She's shrinking, slowly disappearing, beneath it.

Who was she? Where did she come from? How did she learn to do what she did? I'm not sure I'll ever find any answers, but the questions help me make a decision.

Staying low, I back away from the entrance of the cave, crouching behind the spiky bushes to check whether anyone's passing. There's a voice calling out in the distance but I can't see anyone near. I slip out onto the path again and make my way back home, back to where I'm meant to be on the grid.

Seeing her again has strengthened my resolve. Something began the night I found that woman, and it hasn't finished yet.

Mum's still asleep when I come in, one arm draped across her face, the bedcovers pulled high.

I switch the comscreen on but keep it dimmed and mute, checking for messages between Mason and Boc. A new message comes up as soon as I hack into Mason's computer, then soon after, another. They're talking right now.

'We tried, Mase.'

'Yeah. I know.'

Biting my lip, I type the message I've been rehearsing all the way home. 'OK, we can meet. But I choose the time and place.' Then I hit send.

Silence. The seconds blink past on my screen. Fifteen, sixteen, seventeen ...

Mason's reply comes back: '???'

'You know who I am.'

There's another pause, but I know it's just a matter of time. Boc's the one who finally replies. 'Where? When?'

'Entrance gates at Footscray Park, 4pm Friday.'

CHAPTER SIX

SOMEHOW BOC HAS climbed one of the pillars at the park entrance and is sitting on the top of it when I walk up a few minutes after four on Friday.

They both turn my way at the same time, and I have to concentrate on keeping my movements relaxed, fighting back a sudden urge to turn and run. *Be careful, Scout,* I remind myself. *Think about every word.*

I've already swiped the chip's history map clean, of course, but I remember the dates that used to be there pretty well. I've spent some time thinking it through: how many times she skipped, how old I would be for it all to make sense.

Mason stands away from the gate and takes a few steps towards me. 'Thanks for coming. Way cool you're going to help us.'

I shake my head. 'I don't know if I can help, but I'm willing to listen.' I speak slowly and meet his gaze.

He blinks with his mouth pushed to one side as if trying to hide the frustration. 'Fair enough.' It's a start.

By now, Boc has manoeuvred his way down the side of the pillar with the skill of an acrobat. 'Where to?'

'Follow me.'

Together, the three of us make our way down the path and into the park. We catch up to a young couple with a toddler going in slow zigzags, passing them in silence.

'So you know how to hack into messages, I see?' Mason asks when we're out of earshot.

'A bit.'

'How did you learn? I mean, the system was updated last year and you're well up with the coding.'

My steps jolt so suddenly that I almost trip and somehow manage an awkward skip to recover. It's something I haven't even considered in my careful story creation. How would this person I'm supposed to be keep up to date on that kind of thing? 'I'll take that as a compliment,' I say after a moment. As if I'm chuffed rather than caught unprepared.

They glance at me, expecting an answer. My mind races.

'Yeah, it's just … I have an amazing teacher.' Alistair. I don't even have to make this up. 'He's been coding since the twenties and he's brilliant. Taught me everything I know.' I don't even glance at them as I talk, just having a casual chat. 'Most of the coding languages you use today are based on old ones.' This, at least, is true. 'Once you get the basics, it's just a matter of updating each time. You know?'

Finally I risk a peek sideways. Mason has his eyebrows raised, impressed. He bought it.

'How much of our stuff have you seen?' he asks.

It's relief that keeps me casual. 'Not much. You're the ones who started watching me first, remember?'

'Touché,' says Boc. I catch the hint of a smile.

At least the questions have stopped. Halfway to the canal we turn down a section of path near the edge of the park. There's a shady clearing to one side, edged by trees and lined with polyturf. It's the sort of place where you can talk without anyone overhearing.

Mason finds a place to one side, arms hugging his knees, while I find a patch and sit with my legs crossed. It's strange being with them now. After reading their messages and watching them on the grid, I almost feel as if I know these guys. Though, of course, I don't.

Boc does a full circle before settling in front of us. I get the sense he won't be there long. His eyes trace up the trunks around us, maybe working out which ones he can climb.

'So.' Mason rubs his hands together. 'You were born in 2024, but you don't look any older than …' One eyebrow lifts as his he scans my face.

'Fourteen,' I say honestly. There were so many long gaps in the woman's history map that she'd only have aged about three years since the start of the ration system. Unless they saw her in person there's no way they could know she was older than me.

'It must be so weird,' Mason says, eyes still on me. 'How much the world has changed.' We're all quiet before he continues.

'Is there anything you want to know? About, you know, how everything works these days?'

'No, Miya is helping me.' I sit a bit straighter, acting sort of annoyed and proud. 'Listen. I'll help you if I can, but don't expect me to tell you my life story okay?'

'Okay, okay.' Mason's hands go up. 'Whatever you say. I just want some help with time skipping.' His hands drop as I nod in agreement. 'Each time you disappear on the grid, you're re-orienting in time, yes? That's why you return to the same location.'

'That's how it seems.' I glance at Boc, who's sitting quietly, and then back to Mason.

'So how do you make it happen? Do you meditate?'

'Sort of, ah …' I don't have to know what I'm talking about, but I do have to be convincing. A deliberate nod. 'Yes.'

'So is it like your time just sort of stops?' They both look at me and wait. Mason even has his hands clasped together. I get the feeling that I could make out that I was born on the moon and they wouldn't blink.

'Well, I don't think of it as time stopping, exactly,' I say. 'It's more like I'm ignoring every other time except *now*.'

'Yes, yes.' Mason leans forwards. He's so desperate for answers that he doesn't realise I'm just repeating stuff I read on one of the Relative Time Theory sites.

I swivel my legs around and kneel with my feet tucked under me. It's one of the poses for meditation I've seen described on the time travel sites.

'How about if you explain the process you go through?' I say. 'Take me through, step-by-step.'

Mason matches my pose. 'All right. So, it's as if I'm sinking, right? And I can feel … it's hard to explain … like my brain is slowing.' He has this really quiet way of speaking and I find myself leaning forwards to meet every word.

'And it's almost as if I'm outside of time,' Mason keeps going. 'Like I'm observing it … but then –' He trails off and glances at Boc.

'But then … what?'

Mason's reply is a shake of his head.

Boc's head tips back as he studies the tops of the trees. 'Have you tried?' I say to him.

Slowly Boc's chin drops as he considers what to say. 'Meditation wasn't exactly on my radar before this. So I had to come from behind.' He glances at Mason and then hitches himself around to sit facing him with his shoulders square. 'But I'm catching up. Getting better every day. You'll see, I'll get there before you know it.' His tone is defiant, almost challenging.

Mason shuffles closer to me on his knees. 'The thing I don't understand is how did you know it was first possible?'

I shake my head slowly. 'I don't know. It was just a feeling, I guess. It just … happened.' They're both quiet, waiting expectantly, and all I can think of is that woman who died. She's not far from where we are now, alone in the cave.

'I guess I was just trying to survive,' I say quietly.

'Hey, yeah.' This time it's Boc who reacts, pacing forwards

on his knees as he pulls out his compad. 'There was that snap hailstorm a couple of years back. You jumped right in the middle of it. And then the time before, there was that massive dust cloud. I looked it up.'

My mouth opens and I clamp it shut, glad that the other two are busy checking their compads. I'm itching to pull mine out to check as well, but I resist. Why would I check the weather reports from days I'm meant to have lived through?

The other two are busy for a while as my mind ticks over. This is interesting. It makes me think about the woman's blackened fingers. Could that have been frostbite?

'It's like what you were saying,' Boc says to Mason. 'About the way people slow their own time so they can survive. Like when that wall of bricks fell and those kids dodged out of the way.'

'Sure. It makes sense.' Mason shuffles closer on his knees. 'Will you jump for us now? Show us how you do it?'

They're like cats, tracking each tiny movement of their prey.

'You don't have to go far, just a minute or two,' Mason begs.

All I can do is shake my head, turning from one to the other. 'I'm not sure I could do it around strangers –' As if it's their fault. I bite my bottom lip as Mason frowns into thin air, more questions forming.

This is such dangerous territory. I check my compad as if there's some place I need to be. 'Look, sorry. I have to go.'

They both stand up with me. I clear my throat and say, 'I'm sure you'll get there.'

'Thanks,' Mason mumbles, but I hear the rest of what he must be thinking. *Thanks for nothing.*

Boc's standing with his arms crossed. 'We'll walk you out,' he says evenly.

I don't have much choice other than walking with them. We begin to head back in a group, but soon Boc bolts ahead of Mason and me, stopping to grasp a branch that's reaching over the path, testing it with his weight. He must have decided it's not strong enough because then he sprints ahead again.

Beside me Mason walks in silence, both hands in his pockets, his gaze on the ground just in front of him.

'So I'll just keep trying,' he says, almost to himself. 'Meditate every day.'

As we head up the final steep section towards the front gates, I sneak another glance sideways. Mason's a little taller than me, with fine bones and smooth skin. Compared to Boc he's slight, though compared to someone who's lived on half rations all their life, he's a picture of glowing health.

We're nearly at the front gates when we reach a tree to one side of the path that's shaking with the weight of a body clambering up the branches. Boc. By the time we reach its base and come to a stop, the midsection branches are rustling.

It seems rude not to wait with Mason. I glance over to find him watching me again, and quickly look down.

'Will you at least tell me what it's like?' he asks. 'I mean, I've come close I think, and then I get this sense of something ... sucking me down and it's so empty, like nothing else I've felt.'

The hushed tone in his voice is back; it draws my eyes up to meet his. 'How do you mean?'

'I don't know … it feels like a sinkhole pulling me in. I'm not sure I'll find my way out.'

It makes me think about that woman again. The expression on her face … she wasn't at all tense, it was more like complete bliss.

'It's safe, Mason,' I say, hoping I'm right. 'You don't need to be scared.'

His eyebrows go up. 'Will you stay with me? Or … come back later?'

I shake my head. 'I can't.' Can't look him in the eye either, so I squint up to the branches shaking at the top of the tree.

We say nothing as we track Boc's slow descent.

After a while, Mason lets out a snort. 'I've never seen that guy take a backwards step. Like *ever*.' His voice has dropped so low again that I have to turn in order to hear. His head tilts close to me, his eyes moving over mine as he speaks. 'I mean, he's great. Don't get me wrong. But he's the only person I've met who is scared of nothing. He just doesn't get how hard this is. Keeps saying he'll get there first, as if this is easy. That's why I wanted to see you again. To ask for your help.'

It's as if he wants to climb inside my mind, the way he's looking at me, as if I actually count. After being invisible my whole life, this is such a strange place to find myself. It's unnerving, but I kind of like it.

Almost from a distance, I hear myself saying, 'Okay. Tomorrow night.'

His face relaxes into a hopeful smile. 'Where?'

What am I doing? 'Your basement. Eight o'clock.'

I don't want to be stuck with slow train connections on the way home, so I ride my bike to Mason's house. It's not too bad: forty-seven minutes door-to-door.

Mum knows exactly where I am. It's easier since she's met them. She thinks I've come to discuss the entrance interview. Close enough.

Mason welcomes me in, this time looking any place except my face. As I follow him in he points out rooms to fill the silence. We pass a lounge room and he introduces me to his mum. She seems surprised to see me but is otherwise gentle and quiet, somehow like a stranger in her own house.

Mason lists a series of hot concentrates – coffee, tea, hot chocolate – and doesn't react when I refuse. Of course, it would have been rude to accept.

'I've been limiting my food intake?' he says, barely above a whisper. 'I've found I'm more in the moment when I'm hungry?' Each sentence finishes with a question at the end, as if asking for my assessment.

'Yeah, that's good,' I say confidently. 'And maybe not too tired?' I'm talking about study techniques rather than time travel. But who's to know that?

It's become easier now that I've realised that I don't have to actually know about any of this; I just have to be convincing enough to keep Mason believing I do.

'Have you tried waking up early to meditate?' I suggest. It was on one of the sites I was reading.

We're clomping down old wooden stairs and Mason pauses in front of me: 'Your time jumps were at all times of day.' He is matter of fact.

'Yeah, but ...' I stumble for recovery. 'While you're trying to get the feel for it, I mean.'

His head tilts, considering the suggestion as he continues ahead of me.

At the bottom of the stairs is a door that leads into a converted garage, not a basement like I thought. He already has a bedroom upstairs, so it seems insanely luxurious to have this as well, two whole rooms to himself.

Paler bricks fill out the space where the roller door used to be, a long window lining the top. I get the feeling that this was used as a living room when it was first converted; there's a cityscape art print on one wall and a family portrait on the other with Mason, his mum, a man in a beard and a guy that must be Mason's older brother. A sideboard has been dressed with an empty vase.

Layered on top of it all is Mason. A doona lies bunched at one end of a couch, a pillow at the other and a keyboard in easy reach. A comscreen is the focus of the coffee table. You can almost see an outline where Mason spends his time, the glow of the screen lighting a circle around his downstairs world.

'What do you think?' He lifts an arm towards the space.

'Yeah, wow, great!' Until I realise that he's asking whether he could time skip here. A nod as I glance around. Even a chin rub. 'Hmm, should be fine.'

Mason seems to have given up asking me to demonstrate a jump for him. At least, I hope he has. He pulls out an old camping mat and unrolls it on the floor.

'You'll stay with me while I try?' he asks. 'Help me to slow my time?' Mason sits and crosses his legs.

I find a place on the rug a short distance from him. 'Try not to think about it too much,' I say. 'Just feel your way.' He's completely still as I talk, listening to each word. 'Trust that you'll be all right.'

Mason's mouth forms a small oval as he breathes out, hands resting on knees. His eyes slowly close.

'You're going to ah ... reach a place where now is all that exists,' I say calmly, repeating stuff that Mason said in his emails. 'Then you're going to choose a new time to return.'

You can actually see the tension melt away with each breath. The pinch of a frown smooths away slowly. Fingers go limp. Shoulders soften.

His skin is a light golden, face narrow. His frame is slight but balanced.

It's only now that I'm sitting here, with space and time to think, that I realise why I've come. One of the reasons, at least. I'm here to see what they're like, these people my age who were chipped, deemed worthy of the resources to help them live. They have a complete set of mother and father citizens, of course. But still. What makes them special? I want to know. Why were they chosen?

After about twenty minutes, Mason pulls out of the meditation, breathing in and opening his eyes. Complete peace hangs about him. 'I went close, but it's not easy with –'

'With me here?' I finish. Not surprised.

'Yes, but ...' The pinch of a frown is back. 'You helped, too. It felt different. Not so empty.'

Already it's getting weird so I cover up by standing and straightening my shirt.

'Stupid to think that it would work first time,' Mason says quietly. I'm walking to the stairs when he calls out, 'Will you come again?'

I turn. 'Why?'

'I know it's possible because of you.' His face is so open, so trusting. 'You stop me from giving up.'

Still he has faith. I can't help wondering what he'd think if he knew the truth.

'Will you come again?' he pushes.

A pause, but I don't really need to consider. 'Sure.' Because I think I have faith, too.

Even though I don't know how it works, I saw someone jump in front of me so I know it can be done. There's just the small matter of working out how.

CHAPTER SEVEN

I START HANGING OUT with Mason more after that, riding
over to his garage after he finishes school. I'm glad to discover
there's a side entrance, which means I don't have to knock on
the front door. Boc's often there before I arrive, but he never
stays long. It's as if the room is too small for him. There's nothing
for him to climb.

You'd think it would be weird, hanging out with guys my
own age after being stuck on the outside my whole life. But it's
not. Mason's so obsessed that he just picks up from where we
left off the time before; talking through his latest list of theories
or a new idea he's going to try.

I still keep an eye on him online, just in case. One day I find
a document on his hard drive with dates and notes that make
no sense at first. It lists a bunch of numbers and phrases: 4/7/84,
26 deg, 5.5 hr sleep, 930 cal, no carb, 30 min cardio, 5.30pm, 87%.

Under the date when I first went around, he'd added a single word: *Scout.*

He's recording all the conditions that he meditates in, I realise. Exercise, diet, sleep and weather, even his changes in body temperature throughout the day: Mason's been recording his whole life, tweaking his diet, sleep and exercise in case it helps him slow his sense of time. Whenever he reaches a deeper meditation, the different aspects from that day get highlighted and repeated in the next session, until he makes it even closer and refines each one all over again.

I start reading more about meditation as well, and practising at home, allowing myself to sink into the quiet spaces in my mind. I still don't know what I'm doing, but I do know that the answer is out there, somewhere. It's floating just out of our reach, waiting for someone to give it a name.

I'm not expecting to disappear, exactly, but meditating takes me closer to some of the things that Mason's been saying. Here and there while I'm meditating, my thoughts begin to slow, and I feel as if I'm coming to understand what he meant when he said he was outside time.

Once, I even reach a place where I'm suddenly awake and blinking, confused and staring around as if I'd forgotten for a split second who I was. That freaked me way out. Not because I thought I was doing it wrong, but because maybe I'd done something right.

Sometimes I meditate with Mason. It felt weird to me at first, but he didn't seem to notice, and soon I found that it's different from when I'm alone. It brings a deeper focus when we both slow at the same time: the air seems to still, the sounds from outside shrink further away. The focal point of the room becomes sharper somehow.

About three weeks after my first trip to Mason's house, I'm in his garage, grabbing my backpack ready to ride home. It's 5.45pm and already the air is still with cold creeping in from outside.

Mason's on the floor, his legs still crossed after a session that seemed to take both half a day and no time at all. 'Nervous about the interview tomorrow?' he asks simply.

I stop with my zip, frowning as I turn. I haven't even mentioned the test to him, let alone the interview. My mouth has already shaped the words *how did* ... before I realise.

'You've been watching me?' Even now, he's watching me on the grid?

'I keep expecting you to disappear.' If he noticed the protest in my voice, he doesn't show it.

I hook the backpack over my shoulders, ready to get going, but Mason shuffles around so that he's facing me. 'Why haven't you?'

'I told you, I can't do it in front −'

'No, but, on your own. Why have you stopped jumping altogether?'

I'm not sure if he's worried I'm going to disappear, or suspicious about why I haven't. I let one arm drop. The mood in the room seems to have shifted. 'You want me to?'

One eyebrow lifts slightly. 'I just want to know why you

haven't.' He's perfectly still, his face like an elven statue, waiting for an answer.

I sink to sit on the edge of the couch, the backpack drops to the floor. In my mind I track my life back the way Mason thinks it was.

She's fainter now but I can still feel her here, with me. The woman I'll never know.

'Well … I ah … just want to live my life now. I want to get into a good school.' Mason keeps watching, so I keep searching. *This will make sense,* I tell myself. I just have to find a way through. 'It's not easy … being on the move all the time.' And then I find it. 'When I first jumped, I left some people behind. Friends and family. When I came back they were older.'

I finish and my shoulders relax because what I just said has to be true. I've been searching for other people with gaps on the grid, and so far found none.

Mason takes a breath and I expect him to speak, but he pushes his lips together. He takes another go before the words come out: 'Have you ever travelled backwards?'

I've wondered this too, because a gap is only proof that the person disappeared. It could mean that they return at an earlier time, in theory. But once you see that the woman always came back to the same location, it's clear that she only ever jumped forwards, otherwise her line would double back on itself.

I shake my head. 'No.'

'Have you tried?'

Less of a shake this time, because how would I know?

Mason's quiet as he considers. 'It might be possible,' he says softly before looking over again. 'Would you go backwards if you could?'

'I don't know.' I think for a bit. 'It doesn't make sense to me, going backwards. Like, if you travel back and kill your younger self. Except now you're dead, so there's no future self to come back and kill you.' Mason's smiling by now, nodding, so I join in. 'So now you survive, but that means you're alive to come back and kill yourself ...'

'Yeah, yeah.' He's still smiling, but he glances away, almost sad.

'My brain hurts.' I grab the backpack and breathe in as I stand. 'Right now, all I can think about is getting into a decent school.'

Mason stands with me while I walk to the door. 'Listen,' he calls out. 'The way things work these days? It's all about how much you contribute to the state.' I must seem a bit unsure because he keeps going. 'So make sure your plans for the future sound useful, okay?'

'Yeah. Thanks.'

We arrive five minutes early for the interview and have to wait for ages, our backs slowly sagging with each click of the clock.

We're still there when the next interviewee after me arrives with her dad, and our backs snap straight again. She's one of those bouncy people with a ponytail that flicks when she moves. I return her grin nervously and try not to look at her A2 art folio. Architecture, perhaps? Disaster co-ordination?

When it's finally my turn, I'm already on the other side of nervous. We enter the meeting room to find two empty chairs at a round table with about seven or eight people in business suits sitting around the circle. They all have labels in front of them: important community members, school staff and the principal opposite me. I think it's meant to feel inclusive and equal. I just feel sick.

Everyone stands when we come in and I resist the urge to curtsey. It's all so formal. The year nine co-ordinator introduces herself as Ms Leoni and asks us to take a seat.

No-one speaks while we all shuffle into position. I make a point not to let myself focus anywhere near Mum because I know she'll be smiling so hard that I might throw up.

'Coutlyn Roche.' Ms Leoni taps at her keyboard and all faces lean towards their compads. 'Now. Your test scores were good across the board. Very good, in fact. You're starting with the exact broad base that we're looking for. And your references are solid, too.' She pauses to peer at her screen. 'I've had some trouble chasing one of your teachers for a phone reference … Miss Smythe?' She looks over at us. 'Is that it? With a y?'

Mum and I turn to each other: 'Isn't it with an i?'

'I think it's a y but no e.' My heart's beating so hard that I'm sure the guy from Orion Energy sitting next to me is about to ask what the noise is.

We mutter about the spelling some more and then I shake my head. 'Actually, you know what? I just remembered. She got married last year and changed her name.'

'Oh! That explains it.' Ms Leoni smiles. 'What's her married name?'

Her married name, it turns out, is even harder to spell than her maiden name and we only have to disagree twice about the spelling before Ms Leoni tells us not to worry, she'll sort it out. I don't let her know that the only teacher in the city with that name is on an extended holiday.

The whole room relaxes after that. Especially me. A woman from the Disaster Co-ordination Centre keeps nodding at everything I say, so I find myself speaking to her and just glancing around the table here and there.

They ask about my goals after leaving year twelve, and the guy from the CSIRO grunts something like *yaar* when I list the universities that offer Bioengineering.

I'm even able to take a full lungful of air by the time they ask about my hopes for after uni. I have heaps of ideas about ways that food technology might help us feed more people and I'm only at the start when a man at the edge of my sightline shakes his head.

'Feed more people and you'll also have to house them. Not to mention the extra energy and water.' He's skinny with age, red flaky skin. This guy is old.

My eyes flick to the name label in front of him: Minister for Resources and Rationing. I take a breath. 'True, but ... we can find ways to deal with that, too.'

'We already have tighter rationing because of the problems with the Murray Darling. How would we cope with another disaster like '79?' He's talking about the fire that went through the city's water treatment plant. 'Why feed illegals when we already struggle with the citizens we have?'

My lungs have gone empty. I glance at Mum, and immediately turn away. She was gripping her seat so hard that I could see the network of veins in her neck. I try the woman from the Disaster Co-ordination Centre but she offers only a pained smile before glancing down and I'm left staring back at the Minister for Resources and Rationing. Just him and me.

'Try to help everyone, Coutlyn Roche, and you might end up helping no-one.' His voice seems stronger than it should be and I find myself imagining a younger man behind the dry skin and wrinkles.

'But that's no reason to stop trying?' I can't help the little lift at the end: don't you agree?

The Minister slowly clasps his hands together and rests them on the table. His eyes stay on me the whole time.

My lips are dry. I've been breathing through my mouth. I shuffle awkwardly in my chair, searching for an answer.

Why feed illegals? I want to say. *Because we're human beings, that's why. We're meant to look out for each other.*

And because I'm one of them, of course.

The silence has lasted way too long, but I have no idea what to say next.

'The reason to stop trying, Coutlyn,' says the Minister finally, 'is that now more than ever we need to use our resources wisely. And that especially includes our human resources.' He pauses, and I feel the whole panel watching me. 'You and your peers here today are our future, you realise that, don't you?'

I'm not sure if he expects an answer, but I sit taller in the chair and nod as agreeably as I can.

'Some would say that you owe it to your country to work where the need is greatest. Judging from your IP, Coutlyn Roche, I'd say you were best suited to medicine. Or disaster co-ordination, perhaps.'

'Okay.' Still nodding. 'Yes, that would be okay.' It's weird how he keeps using my full name.

'If you spend your time trying to help people that can't be saved, others are placed at risk.'

'I guess. Yes, that makes sense. I could work in medicine.' I'm saying the words but they feel empty.

'Well,' Ms Leoni breathes in and glances around the table. 'Any more questions from the panel?'

Everyone shakes their heads. My eyes stay locked on the Minster for Resources and Rationing as he clicks something on his compad. He lifts his head to examine me again, and crosses his arms.

By now Mum's standing, so I do too, bowing my head and thanking everyone. Then we're out the door into the dusty school grounds and it's all over.

It's over.

Swirls of wind and dirt outside make it difficult to talk, so it's not until we're heading along the train concourse that Mum speaks. 'I can't believe —'

'It'll be all right.' No way I'm going to hear her say it out loud. *You messed up.*

'Yes.' But her head tilts down. 'I'm sure it's fine.'

Neither of us says anything for ages. If she started yelling about the interview, then at least I could yell about it too. But how would that help? Screaming about it isn't going to change anything.

In silence, we let the crowd pull us along. I never imagined that I might mess up the interview. I've been prepping for the test for years, but the interview never worried me. I can't even work out what annoys me more, the fact that I stumbled so badly over my answer or the way I backed down.

As we step through security, I slip a hand into my pocket and grip the lump in the corner, pressing it hard, angrily, into my palm. The sensors go *tuk* as I pass, but somehow the sound has changed.

I used to think that if I could make it into a good school, I'd become a normal citizen. Fit in. But I see now that's not how it's going to work, even if by some freak fluke I still make it in. No matter how many times I swipe that chip, it's always going to belong to someone else. I'm always going to be illegal.

We're almost on the platform when I turn towards Mum. 'Can I go over to Mason's?' Right now, I can't stand the idea of spending the afternoon with her. It would be a constant reminder of the interview.

A pause as she blinks two or three times. 'I guess so.' She seems dazed.

'I'll catch the train home before it gets late.'

'Yes.' Only now does she lift out of her thoughts, placing a hand on my shoulder. 'Watch the weather, okay? Call a taxi if the storm picks up.'

'Yeah.'

Her eyes begin to soften and I spin the other way, her sadness even worse than silence. Numbly, I make my way over to the next platform. School wouldn't have finished yet but I send a message anyway. *Can I come over?*

The reply comes back two minutes after finish time: *Sure.*

Mason's still in uniform when he opens the side door, navy tie tucked into a thick blazer. For a moment I'm unable to speak. I'm not even sure why I'm here. I can't tell him what just happened, not the whole story. I can't say how I really feel.

'Hey.' He steps back to let me in.

A gust of wind bursts up, bringing dust and leaves inside with me. Mason swipes the door shut. 'Crazy day.'

'You can say that again.' I let myself sink to the edge of the couch, my body suddenly heavy.

'How'd it go?'

I manage a shrug. 'Not great. They didn't like my plans to work in food technology.'

'You should take the computing stream. You can pretty much work in any industry from there.'

'Yeah.' A sigh. 'If I get in.'

'Don't worry. You'll be fine.'

He seems so sure. And it's only now that I realise how close to the fire I've been playing. Until the interview I didn't recognise how much being illegal is part of who I am. The way I think, the words I say. I've been living this life for so long that I don't know how to think like a citizen. I thought I could fool everyone, but maybe I've been fooling myself.

'Listen, I've been thinking –'

Mason sits on the armrest across from me, hand resting on one knee.

'– maybe I should stop coming round.'

'What?'

'I'm sorry. It's just ... I really have no idea how it works. I wish I could help you, but I don't think I –'

'No.'

'But maybe I'm making it worse.'

'No,' he says again, a shake of his head. 'Hang on.' Mason slips off the armrest to kneel beside the couch, one elbow on the seat and the other on the coffee table. 'Look, stop coming if you want, but don't do it because I can't time jump.'

My head shakes, a sad smile. The fact is that the longer I hang out with Mason, the closer I come to letting the truth slip out.

'I know why I can't do it, and it's nothing to do with you.' He inhales and turns to tap one finger on the coffee table. 'I'm scared. That's the reason. Not you.'

I know. I knew that already. But still I don't know how I can help.

'Maybe it's just one of those things,' I say after a while. 'Until you do it for the first time, it's always beyond your safety zone. Always the unknown.'

'I've come close,' Mason says. 'But each time I feel it pulling me in, I panic ...'

'It's okay. Maybe one day, when you're ready, it'll just ... happen.'

He shrugs, and moves around to sit on the floor, resting a shoulder against the couch. I flop backwards on the doona and sigh, but with relief this time.

'What if you could do it?' I ask. 'Like, imagine you already knew how. How far would you go?'

He thinks for a bit. 'Only a few seconds at first.' I'm watching him side-on so I only see one cheek lift as he smiles. 'But once I managed that, then it would mean ...' He raises an arm and sweeps the room with it, as if to say *everything*.

I smile back.

'Will you stay with me, just one last time?'

'Sure.'

We settle into our usual places. A gust of wind makes a branch scrape against the outside wall, but it can't touch us in here. The weather outside might be going crazy, but in here we're safe.

I breathe out and close my eyes first, maybe as a way to reassure him that I won't sit here and watch. A slow exhale like a tyre losing air. I accept the peace that comes from sharing a space with someone in silence.

I let myself sink, allowing thoughts to come and then letting them go, drifting into a place where each second seems to tick past slower than the first. I've been resting inside my mind for a while, when a memory fragment hits me – the Minister for Resources and Rationing crossing his arms – and the whole day comes back with a rush. I am sucked out of the peace in an instant.

It helped a little, though. I open my eyes, glad to have escaped life for a while.

Mason's across from me, his head dropped at an angle, his eyes still closed. I check his chest because I've noticed that the rate that he's breathing seems to match how deeply he's gone in. At first it shows no movement at all, but soon his chest expands and sinks again with a breathy sort of rumbling noise.

A snore, I realise. He's asleep.

The next one grows louder, and with it comes a sudden inhale as Mason's eyes open. 'Wha?' He looks around, and rubs his cheek. 'What was that?'

I hold back a giggle, not very well. 'You umm …' The laugh tries to push out again, so I mush my lips together. 'You fell asleep.'

He barely reacts, other than becoming a little pinker. For some reason that makes me giggle again, and this time even Mason doesn't seem able to hold back. A couple of shy snorts from him set me off. Laughter bubbles up from his stomach and into his chest until it escapes.

'Sorry,' Mason says once the laughter dies. 'Sorry about that.'

'No worries.' I'm expecting that to be the end, but for some reason he breathes out and shuts his eyes again. His shoulders relax, fingers softening once more.

A few seconds later, there's a faint rush of air and his clothes fall to the floor.

He's gone.

CHAPTER EIGHT

I DON'T BREATHE AS the seconds tick past. My brain won't compute what it's seeing. Mason's not here.

Moments later, the empty space fills with his form and a sob rises in my throat. He's here again, except naked, sitting cross-legged on top of his clothes.

I'm stunned, speechless. He was gone, and now he's back. My eyes trace the shape of each muscle and take in the smooth shade of his skin. He's even slimmer than I imagined. His arms and chest are toned and lithe.

I glance away, my cheeks and neck warming at the intimacy of seeing him like this. But then my eyes move back again. He doesn't seem to have noticed his nakedness. His head is tilted back, lips parted slightly.

I've seen that expression before …

It's only as his lips kink up at the corners that it hits me. It's the exact same expression I saw on the woman after I'd just discovered her: complete and utter bliss.

A sucking gasp is the first sound that comes from Mason, like a skindiver who's just broken through the water's surface.

'Oh my holy cripes! That was *freaking amazing*.' As he speaks, his eyes open and he looks down to take in his bare skin. He looks over at me, beaming. 'No wonder you didn't want to jump in front of us.'

With a push onto hands and knees, he crawls forwards. One hand reaches around to cup my neck. The next thing I know, Mason is leaning closer, closer and pressing his lips against mine.

My eyes blink and I let them shut, feeling the flush of heat from his skin. He pushes forwards as if thirsty for more. His lips taste of butter and salt.

Mason pulls away, still grinning, and it's only when he sees my surprise that the spell is broken.

'Wow. Sorry.' His hand pulls away.

'No, no, it's okay –'

'I've never kissed anyone like that before. It's just … you know how amazing this feels.'

'It's okay,' I try again, but it barely comes out a whisper.

His face softens and he brushes the backs of his fingers against my cheek.

'It's just … I mean, this changes *everything*.' By now Mason's standing, picking up his jeans and laughing when he sees that the buttons are fixed in their holes. 'This proves that it's a natural process, something we can learn to do.' He loosens the buttons and steps into the legs before pulling them up.

They're barely over his hips when he begins pacing, too full of everything to stay still. Words stream out of him, fragmented and barely formed, as if a microphone has been plugged into the centre of his brain:

'It must be lying dormant in every human being. Waiting ...

'Now that I know how it feels ...

'... just have to escape the limits of our minds. It's our fixed ideas that hold us back.'

Mason's pacing has only just begun to slow when I receive a message from Mum: *Taxi on the way*. It's not too late for me to catch the train home, but the storm has just broken and rain on the roof is drowning the other sounds.

A taxi pings its arrival a few minutes later, and Mason walks me to the door. He cups my head in his hands as if he's going to kiss me again but he just grins. It's sort of contagious, so I grin back.

'This is so freaking amazing, Scout,' he calls over the noise of the rain. 'Thank you so, so much.' He reaches around to hold me in a hug before pulling back. 'Tomorrow. Yes?'

'Yes,' I say, though I'm not sure anymore what tomorrow even means.

I'm glad for the chance to sit in the taxi, tucked away while the lights streak past in the rain. Safe in the dark, I lift a hand to my mouth and allow myself a secret smile.

Soon I hear a clunk as the taxi drops into deceleration and turns off the highroad into the streets near our house. We're travelling slowly enough to see out properly now, and as we reach the end of my street we pass Kessa and her twin sister racing towards their front porch, backpacks raised as shelter.

How very strange. The whole world has burst open, become something entirely new, and they have no idea.

I float through the front door and into our room, confused and happy and scared all at once. It's as if I've just heard the high notes of a song I'm going to love for the rest of my life.

Mum's in one of the armchairs, resting her head in a hand, her face flickering cool blue from the comscreen. She turns to me slowly and yawns before flicking it off. 'Have you eaten?'

'No.' I'm still floating. No need to sit. 'I'm not hungry.'

'Sure?'

'Yes.' No need to eat.

Mum stands, and stretches her chest and arms. 'All okay?' She smiles when I nod, and stretches again. 'Listen, Scout? You did the right thing, all right? There's no shame in telling them what they want to hear.'

It takes me a while to return to the world I left only hours ago. Before …

Mum's still going. 'Once you have a place in the school, you'll be able to make your own choices. I thought you handled it well. Sometimes you have to say what they want to hear.'

'But I …' Only now do I finally catch up. 'I messed up. I thought you were upset.'

'Nooo.' Mum slips an arm around my shoulders and squeezes. 'Definitely not upset. Not with you, at least.' She lets go and sinks into the armchair again. 'They think they have the right to control everything, but you can't treat people like that. It doesn't work.'

She's thinking of Dad, I'm pretty sure. Once he stopped being useful, they sent him away.

'I was annoyed by the way that man shouted you down,' Mum finishes.

I hook a knee over an arm of the other chair and sit sideways so that I'm facing Mum. 'You think I still have a chance?'

A pause. 'Yes. I do.'

Then we go quiet, and I imagine that we're thinking about the same things. How getting into school any other way is impossible for me. How the first step in applying for jobs is your academic record. I've tried already to forge a transfer from another school, as well as copy and change an academic record, but those things are encrypted and password-protected tighter than the national security secrets, especially now that knowledge is currency.

'And don't forget second round offers,' Mum says after a bit.

I don't want to keep talking about it, so I just say, 'Yeah.'

Mum sinks into a longer yawn. She gets tired earlier and earlier these days. 'Ready for bed?'

A single shake of my head. 'Might stay up a bit. I'll be quiet.'

'Don't think I'll hear a thing, I'm bushed.' Mum kisses me on the forehead before slipping out for the communal bathroom. I watch the latest episode of Top 40 while she's getting ready for bed and then switch it off when she calls goodnight.

I don't even bother with a lamp, just sit here in the dim light reaching through the cracks in the blind from next door, listening as her breathing softens and slows. She's asleep in minutes.

I'm alone with my thoughts again. I slip off the armchair and onto the floor, aware of the solid feel of the floorboards beneath me. Legs crossed, hands resting on knees. A steady exhale. Maybe I'll never understand the science of it, but seeing Mason skip ahead those few seconds has brought the truth of it into focus. It's as if we've discovered some strange sea-creature that's been living in the deepest caves of the ocean, or stumbled across a universal law that explains the expanding of the planets.

Another breath, and I let myself sink. I still feel like I'm feeling my way towards a place I've never been, but it's easier now. The finish line is there waiting, somewhere ahead of me.

There's no sense of a sinkhole the way Mason described. It's more as if I've been washed into a never-ending tunnel, my senses dulled and my thoughts mute as I drift. There is a place deep within me where now is the only time that exists.

For some reason I'm tired when I pull out, not refreshed at all. But I know I came closer than ever.

The difference this time, I suppose, is that I've begun to believe that maybe I can do it too.

Mason calls the following afternoon, asking when I'll be there. It's a question of 'when' rather than 'if'. I'm not sure whether I should go, but I also doubt anything could stop me.

He's still beaming when he opens the door; I imagine that

he's had the same look on his face since I left yesterday. He pulls me into a victory bear hug.

'So I've been reading up,' Mason says over my shoulder before pulling back. 'We all have these interval timers in our brains. They're part of the body clock network, except these ones help us create our own sense of time. Can you control the exact time you return?' He lets go of my shoulders and finally pauses for breath.

'Ah … sometimes.'

'And guess what? I did it again this morning. Eight seconds. Think I'm getting a feel for it.'

Mason turns to the comscreen on the coffee table, and it's only now that I realise we're not alone.

Boc. 'Longest bloody seconds of my entire life,' he says over the top of the screen. 'And then I copped an eyeful when he came back. Almost gave me a heart attack.'

Mason turns back to me, still grinning. 'At least we know why she wouldn't jump in front of us.' He's staring at me the same way he did last night, as if we're forever linked. For some reason it makes me blush and look away.

'The feeling's mutual, Scout, in case you're wondering,' Boc calls, his eyes back on the comscreen. 'No way my first jump will be in front of you.'

Mason does an about-face and starts pacing like an army cadet. 'I know what you mean about it being gut feel. I get it now. You can't overthink it, you have to feel your way in.' Part way across the room, he turns back to face me.

Finally he falls quiet, his eyes resting on me softly as if deep in thought and I can't help wondering if we're thinking the same thing. *About last night …*

'Yeah, I think you've got it,' I say honestly. I'm in the presence of a guy who worked out the secret to time travel.

'Well, what do you know,' Boc declares, raising his eyebrows at Mason.

'You found her?' Mason makes his way to the comscreen and wedges a foot on the armrest.

I make my way round the back of the couch. 'Found who?' On the screen is the grid in real time, zoomed in far enough to see a single dot moving slowly along one edge of a long room.

'New cleaning lady at school.' Boc zooms in so close that we can see her travelling slowly up the screen. 'Someone noticed that she never orders lunch in the cafe. Always brings it in.'

'And skipped lunch the other day,' says Mason.

'So?' I'm balanced over the back of the couch, tipping forwards slightly.

'So we thought she might be illegal,' says Boc. 'You can tell because they don't come up on the grid. They're not chipped.'

I take in the screen again. The dot's nearly at the end of the room. 'But that's her, isn't it? That person's chipped. You're sure that's her?'

'Yeah, I found the cleaning roster on the school's system. So I knew where she would be. And that's her wing all right. Room 11C.'

I let myself sink low so that my chin and forearms are the only parts of me resting on the back of the couch, a protective barrier of sorts.

In silence we stare, mesmerised by the dot.

'What if you couldn't find her on the grid?' I ask, still watching. 'What if she wasn't chipped?'

'Well ...' Mason and Boc exchange a look. 'We'd eyeball her in the real world first, make sure we had it right.'

'Remember that skinny kid at the tip?' Mason asks Boc, before turning to me. 'That's what we were doing when we first noticed your gaps. Want a drink?'

I shake my head, but can't help following him. I end up standing in the middle of the room, anchorless somehow. 'So did you find what you were looking for?'

'Just that once, at the tip. The rest of the time the grid proved us wrong.'

'And what happened?'

'What happened when?'

'With the person who you found that wasn't chipped?'

'We did what anyone would do,' Boc says. 'Called the Feds.'

I try to act as if this conversation is no big deal, but my blood has gone cold.

'What?' This from Boc.

'Nothing.' I clamp my lips together, but not for long. 'I don't know. You don't feel guilty?'

'Why should I?' Boc shakes his head.

'Not at all.' Mason sips from the can and swallows. 'I mean, look at you. You're the reason we ration, so we can nurture the people who will make a difference, make sure they reach their potential.' A pause while he sips again. 'Like … imagine if you weren't a citizen. You'd land in a new time with no rations, no way to survive. We might never have worked out that time skipping is even possible.' His eyes go wide to show how crazy that would be.

My lips push together again, holding back a retort. 'But … that only works in hindsight, doesn't it? I mean, how can you tell who will make a difference and who won't?'

'That's just where we have to trust the system.' Mason lifts a hand as if that's obvious.

They're both watching me, not the screen. I breathe in. Remind myself that they were trying to catch someone else, not me. 'Yeah. It's just … I feel sorry for them, I guess.'

'Well, if you're looking for a charity case, Scout? Here's one.' Boc waves a hand, switching the comscreen to standby, and stands up from the couch.

'I'm the only one here who can't time skip. Think you can work out why?'

———————————

The three of us start meditating after that. Mason gets so excited that he does most of the talking as we go in. Staying quiet and telling Boc that he'll get a feel for it seems to be all that's needed from me. And anyway, each time Mason disappears, the shock and sheer mystery of it overshadows all else.

He's able to do it every time now, reaching that place of deep focus just a bit faster, staying away a touch longer. Already he's able to make nearly a full minute. That might not sound like much, but it's a long time to sit through, with nothing for me and Boc to do other than watch the compad stopwatch race through its digits.

Of course Mason's naked whenever he returns, but it's become so normal that it's not as big a deal as you might think. He always reappears with his legs crossed, the same as when he went in, and the talk is always about how much time has passed, how he felt. In the strangest of ways, it's become so natural that I don't even look the other way.

Other things have changed, too. When Boc first watched Mason time skip, he'd get all energised. He used to ask a heap of questions, but not so many anymore. These days he seems to like it less and less. His breathing grows louder as we wait, a sort of fug of annoyance growing about him the longer he takes to learn. Each second that ticks past is one second more that he's been left behind.

Of course, I know how that feels exactly.

———————————————

Mason asks me over on a Saturday afternoon about three weeks after he first time skipped. It gives me a flip inside followed by a flash of nerves when I realise we're on our own. Boc's on a mountain biking trip out of the city, and he's taken my safety net with him.

'So, I have an idea.' Mason taps a whiteboard that's been propped upright on the floor, and then leans to adjust the stand. 'I got you this.'

'A whiteboard?'

'Yeah.' Mason crosses his legs to sit behind it and motions for me to do the same on the other side. A grin once I'm settled, just his head visible over the top. 'What do you think?'

All I can think to do is lift my eyebrows in a vague sort of shrug.

'A fix for, you know, the clothing issue.'

My eyebrows drop into a frown. 'You want me to time skip behind this?'

'Yeah, listen. I know it's weird. Trust me, I know.' All I can see is Mason's head above the screen. 'But what do you think?'

'I don't know, it's a little ...' thinking fast, '*low* don't you think?' I have to be careful as anything with this.

'Low?'

It was the only excuse I could think of. 'I mean. It's just ...' Maybe if I talk slow enough I'll come up with a reason not to do this. 'I'm not even sure if I can do it with someone else around.' Yes. That's it. 'I've only ever time jumped on my own.'

'Well, why don't we try?'

And straight away, I'm back with nothing to say.

'Listen, Scout.' Mason crawls around to my side of the screen and settles with his knees facing mine. We're really close, but not actually touching. 'I've been working some stuff out, training myself to wake at certain times of the night without using alarms. I reckon that's the key to all this. I mean, think about it, if we can take control of our interval timers, the next step is jumping together.'

He pauses but I don't look up, just focus on the faded denim of his jeans.

'It's like you said,' Mason keeps going. 'Jumping on your own means that you end up leaving people behind, but imagine if we could synch our return …'

When he goes quiet again I can't help lifting my head. It gives me away with the slightest shake.

Confusion shadows his face. 'We don't have to go far. Just a few seconds …'

My eyes drop again. I know how dangerous this is.

'Why not, Scout? I know you were on your own, but you're not anymore. And this is the most amazing … *sensational* thing I've ever known. Don't you want to play with it? Find out how much control we have? Or how far we can push?' With each sentence he inches further into my sightline until I'm forced to focus on his face, acknowledge the hope in his eyes.

What can I say? I'd do anything to say yes.

'I mean, what if we can find a way to go *backwards*?' Mason's peering up at me, head to one side and eyebrows raised. 'Don't you want to try?'

But all I can do is pull away: 'I'm sorry, Mason. I *can't*.'

Mason leans away, his head straightening and his eyes hardening as he registers the words I said.

I think my heart has stopped.

'Can't or *won't*?'

All I can do is shake my head.

We're left staring at each other. Mason's forehead pinches, and he turns away.

He thinks I've rejected him, I realise with a breath. But then my throat goes tight. *He thinks I've rejected him.*

'I have to go.' There's no air left in me, but somehow the words come out. Already I'm standing, blindly grabbing my bag. Escape is all I can think of.

At the door, I pause and glance back: 'See you.'

'Bye.' He hasn't moved. He's still sitting in the same place, facing the space on the floor where I used to be.

―――――――――

At home I gulp down a glass of water, my heart still thudding at how close I just came. If he ever realises I can't time skip …

I've been meditating on my own every day, sinking into the quiet spaces of my mind and feeling my way into the silent tunnel. It's not so much about taking control of time as letting it go.

My mind is spinning right now, but I have to try. I find a place on the mat, and breathe out. My shoulders relax as I let go, drifting down until I'm deep inside. It's cold down here, in this dull-mute place. There's no light and no air. No wonder Mason found it difficult at first.

Mason.

The next thing I know I'm out with a rush, sucked back by the mess of today. I take in the world around me, rubbing warmth back into my arms as if to remind myself that I exist.

My eyes close at the disappointment. *Come on, Scout. You can do this.*

You have to.

CHAPTER NINE

I'M HEADING OUT to collect our delivery on Monday night when I catch Alistair carrying his box back to his room.

He sees me in the hallway, and lifts his chin. 'Any news, Agent X?'

'Not yet.' A slow sigh. 'Should be soon.' I've tried hacking in to the Karoly High School server, but all I could find was a list of applicants and their contact details. 'They said I'd receive a response either way.' Think I added that last bit more for myself than Alistair.

His chin drops. 'Be sure to let me know.' He straightens his back, steadying himself to keep walking along the hall.

I shuffle forwards as if to block his way. 'So, how are you doing?'

'Still working.' A pause, as his eyes come to understand and rest on me. 'How are you?'

'Good.' I check for Mr or Mrs Richardson and decide the

coast is clear. I drop my voice just in case. 'What would you say if I told you that the stuff I was telling you about Relative Time Theory was true?'

Alistair's bushy eyebrows go up, but it's more about paying attention than actually believing.

'I can prove it.'

More of a reaction this time: a jerk of the head, but it's tinged with disbelief. 'You can choose where you are in time?' Alistair asks slowly.

'No. Not me, yet.' I push down the frustration. I've spent all of this past week meditating but each time I come close, I seem to get stuck. It's like I can't find a way out the other side. 'But … I've seen it happen.'

Even as I'm saying the words, I can tell Alistair has barely heard them. They don't carry the weight that I thought they would.

'Scout, listen.' Alistair shifts the weight of the box in his hands. 'Be careful, yes? If I were considering a candidate for my elite school, I'd do some background checks. Do you understand?'

Then again, why would Alistair understand the news I just told him? Unless he actually saw a time skip for real, there's no reason for him to believe that it's possible. Maybe I should show him the gaps on the grid …

'Scout,' Alistair says, a little louder. 'Those sites you've been reading, and all the hours you spend on the grid. If I can see what you're doing, then other people can see it, too. Even with a firewall set up, there are ways around it.'

I frown, not bothering to hide my disappointment. He didn't even listen. 'So you're saying –'

'I'm saying that you need to clear your cache more often. And any reading of the grid history. Be careful what you get up to. At least until you hear back from the school.' He's leaning really close, frowning at me.

'Okay,' I manage. There doesn't seem to be anything else to say.

Alistair draws himself straighter before moving off again. 'Let me know, Agent X,' he calls once he's further up the hall.

I watch as he shuffles away. 'Thanks, Alistair.'

He has a point, I guess. If Mason and Boc taught me anything about hacking, it's that other people can do it, too.

Mum's not due for another half an hour, so I leave our grocery box on the bench and switch the comscreen on. Now that I'm looking, I can see what Alistair was saying. I've been so busy watching Mason and Boc that I haven't been thinking about anyone else checking me. Like the school admin, perhaps.

It's easy to clear stuff from the front end, but harder to swipe it all completely from the mainframe. I'm still picking through the back end, manually selecting and deleting parts of my browsing history, when the corner of the screen pings to show a new message. Only a few words of the message can be seen in the box, and at first my eyes just brush over them. '… pleased to offer …'

My focus zaps to the box, which opens at my blink: 'Congratulations. Your application has been successful. We are pleased to offer you a place at Karoly High School for 2085.'

The message goes on to talk about the uniform, booklist and orientation days but I barely take any of it in. I'm reading it through for the second time when the door slides open.

'Heya.' Mum steps into the room.

I turn to her but no words come. Instead, I dissolve into tears.

Each morning when I wake there's a moment when I remember. It brings a delicious lift, reminding me who I am now: a normal teenager enrolled in a real school. It's everything I've ever dreamed and more.

Life gets busy after I accept the offer: uniform orders, subject selection, downloading various apps and education programs.

I even call Mason, gushing about getting in. 'Can't wait until term starts!' I finish happily.

A pause, before he says, 'That's great, Scout.' But that's all he says.

'What's wrong?'

'I don't know. Guess I didn't expect you to be calling me.' It's as if he expected to never hear from me again.

I want to reassure him, but I can't let him think that I'm ready to skip with him yet. 'Yeah ... I just wanted to tell you I made it.' I decide to leave it at that. 'Anyway. Better go.'

Mum and I go out for dinner to celebrate. The week after, we take Alistair out to the movies. He's part of the reason why I've made it, even though none of us say it directly. Without the stuff he taught me, I never would have worked out how to access the national curriculum lessons online.

Alistair doesn't say anything about Relative Time Theory or my browsing history, but it would have been easy enough for him to check how much I cleared away. During the ads at the start, Mum and Alistair discuss the peace talks in Egypt while I check out the other people in the cinema, and it almost feels as if we're a family of citizens – grandfather, mother and daughter – every one of us sure of our place and worthy of our rations.

The best part about getting into school by far has been the change in Mum. She's been busy sorting out the safest route for me to travel to school, drilling me about our emergency alert plan and working out the best way to have the chip inserted. She seems younger somehow, her movements lighter. And there's something in her eyes that I've never really seen before. Hope.

It's the best feeling, seeing her like that. Especially since I know that she has more good stuff coming. Every morning for the past couple of months I've been transferring credits into a savings account. Already I have enough for a haircut in a real salon and, judging by the speed I'm saving, I'll have enough to add a movie and dinner, too. This year, Mum's going to have the best birthday in the universe.

A few weeks after I received the acceptance, we're called in for ID photos. Everyone has them already, of course, but unless they take the photo themselves there's no guarantee that it won't be doctored in some way. You can't be too sure what anyone's been up to these days.

They have a heap of info sessions, too, about study techniques, online safety and the emergency procedures in a disaster event, and that's before they even mention the extracurricular stuff like clubs and activities. The careers auditorium gets the biggest crowds.

The line for ID photos is the longest I've ever seen. At first I just stand and shuffle, letting the normalness wash over me. After about twenty minutes though, the sense of gratitude begins to fade, even for me. The guy in front of me cranes to see the front as if he thinks that will somehow make it go faster. Then he turns to check out the line behind us, which I'm pretty sure is growing at a faster rate than the line ahead is moving.

The senior band is playing up the front of the hall, which helps pass the time for a while, but we're still a good distance from the front when they stop for a break, and we're left once again with the dull murmurings of the catatonically bored.

I'm tracking the line ahead in my own private form of self-torture when my eyes land on a face staring back at me. She's so out of context that it takes a second to realise who she is, but almost immediately I do a double take. I know the shape of those eyes, have seen her even skin so many times before. It's Kessa, one of the twins who live at the end of our street.

For some reason my cheeks burn and I find myself blinking as if I've been caught naked or something. I look away to cover my surprise.

Pretend to be bored, I tell myself. *Act like you didn't see her.* Her twin mustn't have made it in, which is no surprise. Kessa was always the one with something to prove. But now that my focus has shifted, I wish I hadn't looked away. I'm so used to hiding my truth from people, that I don't know how to react like a normal person. I should have smiled, at least.

I must have been six when I started hacking into the grid so I could catch the twins and their mum on the way to the park. Whenever they went, I just happened to turn up, too. There was always enough of a jumble of parents and carers there that I just made out as if my mum was part of crowd, rather than working on the other side of the city.

It got to the point where Kessa started looking out for me. We'd spend half the time refusing to get off the swings and the other half making stuff out of leaves and polychips to sell at our make-believe shop.

We became so close that her mum started asking who my mum was and whether I'd like to come over to their place for a play. I was still trying to work out a safe way to say yes when Kessa asked if I wanted to do a friend link.

Never in my life have I wanted anything as much as I wanted that. Even riding on the fast train was nothing in comparison. But all I could do was shake my head because without a chip of my own, how could I?

Kessa backed off after that. I'm sure she thought she'd misunderstood how close we were.

The reality was the exact opposite. Kessa was the only friend I ever had.

We've never talked much since then, just an awkward wave in the street every now and then, so I'm not sure what she thinks of me now.

Still acting as if I haven't noticed her, I check the back of the line again. It's stretching out the main auditorium doors by now, the end out of sight. Somehow, that makes it worse; there's no way to anchor yourself in a line when you can't see the end. It makes me think of entering the tunnel when I meditate; the way it feels to be left with no certain future because there's no past to hold you from behind.

When I turn back to the front, Kessa is facing my way again. Somehow I find the courage to meet her gaze and immediately her eyes relax and crinkle. One hand lifts to waist height and three fingers flutter in the faintest of waves.

Pushing aside all doubt, I lift my hand to exactly the same height as hers, a mirror-image hello. Is it possible to miss someone you hardly know? Maybe it's because she's the friend I never had, part of a life that should have been mine, but wasn't.

And yet, here I am, in a line with her. A chip stashed in my pocket. My whole face breaks into a grin as I watch Kessa leave her place and shuffle my way.

'Heeey!' A wink as she slips in next to me so we're shoulder to shoulder.

'Hey.' Can't help pointing at her place. 'Don't lose your spot, you were nearly at the front.'

One shoulder jerks. 'Doesn't matter. It's better with company.'

There's a second of silence, standing side by side, but it's not awkward. More like a nod to the moment.

'Here we are, hey?' I say. 'Who would have thought? Congrats for making it.'

Her whole body sort of relaxes then, her feet shifting position. 'Yeah. Congrats yourself.' She checks the line as if taking it all in from this fresh perspective. 'All these people. And this is just the ones who made it.'

'Yeah.'

'I wonder how many people missed out.'

'I heard about 900.' Because that's how many names were on the rejected list when I hacked in.

'Wow.' She stares at me for a second before her mouth snaps shut. 'Glad I didn't know that before.'

We shuffle ahead, enjoying the hope that comes with moving for a couple of steps before everything comes to a stop and our shoulders sag again.

Another sigh. 'How long now, do you think?' she asks.

'Don't know.' I check the line in front, and make a face. 'Twenty minutes maybe.'

Her head drops back, mouth open in a groan. 'This is worse than the test.'

'You reckon? Nothing's worse than the test. Well, maybe the interview.'

'Tell me about it.'

She leans closer, her voice drops and we spend the next five minutes comparing our interviews. She can't remember the Minister for Resources and Rationing, but it turns out that her story isn't so different from mine. She was told that she's better suited to emergency triage rather than paediatrics, which is sort of the same thing that happened to me. Maybe I didn't stand out as much as I feared.

Chatting this way seems to have helped pass the time because by the next check, we're nearing the front of the line. Suddenly it's as if time shot ahead too fast; I don't want this to end.

'Hey, Kess? Can I ask a favour?'

'Sure.'

I drop my gaze. 'Do a friend link with me?' I keep going as she reacts, talking faster to explain. 'Sorry, I know it's dumb. It's just so that we can meet up on the first day. You can say no.' Does she remember the last time?

'Of course, that'd be great.' Kessa leans close and places a hand on my shoulder. She seems so open, so natural about this, that I can't help wondering how it must feel to have lived a life where linking up is so easy.

Already Kessa has the back of her wrist lifted, ready for mine. One hand in my shirt pocket, I make a loose fist as I press the chip into my palm with my middle finger. Am I standing too stiffly?

Kessa cheers as we tap our wrists together. We're way too old for this, but still it's fun. I make a point of keeping my arm moving then pushing my hand back into a pocket, making sure Kessa never has a chance to focus on the strange way I hold my hand or realise that my 'scar' smudged when our skin touched.

I'll be able to message her now. And she'll be able to message me. Who would have thought? It's as if I've caught up a little bit more to the life that should have been mine.

We reach the front of the line after that and I watch Kessa pose for her photo. Then we wave and head our separate ways. And even though the friend link was immature, as I head home I can't help feeling as if I've made it through to the other side of something. I'm leading a life conjured up from dreams, where hope has become reality.

As I step off the train and move with the crowd towards the exit, I find myself thinking about the way the line for the ID photos moved so slowly at first, and then the way a friendly face made the time speed up.

That was it, in real life. My time moving at different speeds.

I'm still on a high when I come home, singing along to the Indie Top 10 as I whip up Mum's favourite veg and lentil soup. She's really happy too, talking about a breakthrough with one of her clients, and for a moment I'm tempted to drop a hint about her birthday. I feel like knowing that you have something good coming makes the waiting more fun, but the right moment doesn't come and I don't push it. The evening's so good that I just let it be.

I'm not sure that I'll sleep or even that I want to let the day go, but I drift off easily and find myself dreaming of meeting up with Kessa on the first day of school. It's one of those dreams where you sort of know that you're dreaming but you ignore the fact because you don't want to break the magic of it.

After we meet up the dream jolts ahead to the end of the first day. As we're both saying 'See ya tomorrow', I get this *maybe* sort of feeling, like a whiff of possibility ... *maybe, I can*. And even though I know at the back of my mind that I still can't jump ahead in time, in my dreaming mind I decide to try.

Why wait until tomorrow morning to meet up with Kessa again?

In a dreamy fog I close my eyes and let my mind sink. It's the best feeling, even though it's only a dream, and I get this brilliant sense of control over everything, like the way it feels the first time you ride a bike without training wheels. The world has become layered with possibility.

Dream-skipping to the next morning at school is as simple as anything. But even so I get a floating kind of lift as I see that I've done it ...

... when suddenly I'm sucked back up to the surface. A wave of reality washes over me as I open my eyes for real.

It's night. I'm breathing hard and I'm hot all over.

A gasp and I sit up, peering in the dim light at my pale legs. Light engulfs my mind and air hits my lungs. I'm naked and on top of the bedclothes. They're not scrunched at the bottom like I've kicked them off; they're flat beneath my body. But I don't need those clues; already I understand what happened because of the way it feels. It's as if every cell in my body was sleeping and has suddenly zapped to life.

My heart is beating at a million miles a minute as if making up for lost time.

In some ways, it is.

I feel an urgent need to tell someone; to share what I've just done. I reach out for Mum without thinking, then pull back and bite my knuckle. My eyes focus on her outline. One arm is draped across her face, the way she always sleeps. Her cheeks have filled out these past weeks, but her skin still seems pale.

How can I tell her what just happened? I wouldn't know what to say, not without freaking her out.

It's only now that I've done it that I realise how natural this is. I've been time travelling in my dreams all my life. In a dream, you just think about moving ahead, and that's where you go.

I consider calling Mason, but what would I say? I just time skipped for the first time in my life?

My mind's moved to Alistair when I realise that as amazing as that was, I still haven't managed to do it on purpose. I'm closer now than I ever have been before, but …

Can I do it again?

It's 1.34am, but that doesn't stop me. I've never felt more awake as I pull on a pair of jeans, wrap myself in a coat and leave a note for Mum.

Outside it's crisp and quiet, one of those perfect still spring nights. Cars pass here and there but otherwise I'm on my own. The chip is still in its envelope beside my bed. I'd set off an alarm if I brought it with me to Footscray Park, but I've brought my compad. It's a while since I last used the crossing bot, but it still works.

I slip through my usual gap but turn the opposite way, tracking down the edge of the path until I'm not far from the canal. Being here makes me think about the woman in the cave. She did a split second skip in front of me, I'm sure she did. Maybe the blankets hadn't had time to collapse as she disappeared because her jump was so short, barely a fraction of a second.

You can hear sounds of life down here, near the water. Birds, hidden in nests, I imagine. A possum, perhaps. I'm not sure where the noise is coming from but it doesn't make me nervous. We're not so different, them and me. None of us is chipped.

I've done this before, heading out to the park at night, but everything feels new as I find a clearing and settle in, back straight and legs crossed. The coat does a decent job of keeping me dry against the dew.

Eyes closed, I draw in the fresh night air. With the calmest certainty I know that I'm close to the place where now is all that exists.

It's so easy to let go. No need to push, no need even to breathe. All is quiet as I sink into infinity.

In silence I float forwards with my mind, blindly patting at the walls of time, not sure where to go or even who I am.

Until I feel the pull of return.

And I remember.

In a rush I'm back, bursting through the surface of now, light filling my mind. The earth is firm and my body suddenly heavy as I reconnect with the world.

Air fills my lungs as I'm smacked with the high of my first heartbeat, the first rush of blood. Every cell is buzzing, each moment fresher and newer than I've ever known.

My skin tingles. I'm flushed hot and naked, sitting on a pile of clothes and smiling up to the night sky. I did it – on purpose this time.

———————

The next day, I call Mason.

CHAPTER TEN

'MY FIRST TIME was a complete fluke,' I tell Mason. We're in a cafe courtyard near his house, sipping at coffee from icy glasses.

Mason nods, catching a drip of coffee down the side of his glass with his tongue.

'The truth is,' I keep going, 'I first jumped in my sleep. In a dream, actually. I wasn't trying to, it just happened. I never even imagined it was possible before then.'

I need to do this. This is my chance of starting again, this time with the truth. Rebooting, I guess.

'I don't know how it works and especially how to control the point I return,' I explain. 'So that's why I can't answer the stuff you ask me. I really have no idea. I'm not the groundbreaking time traveller you think I am.' Maybe he'll never know the whole of it, but at least I can tell him this much.

'*Scout* ...' Mason's head tilts as his eyes soften. 'You don't need to be ashamed. Why didn't I think of that? Finding your way into the sinkhole really is a lot like dreaming, hey?'

I lean closer, my forearms on the table. That's exactly how it felt in the tunnel last night, moving through the timeless realm of the subconscious.

'Do you know what this means?' Mason pushes the glass to one side and matches my pose. 'If it happened by accident then it means I'm right, it really is a natural process. I mean ... it makes sense, doesn't it? A bird doesn't need to understand aerodynamics in order to fly.' He pulls away and arches his back. 'This is good news. For all we know time skipping has been available all along and we just didn't recognise –'

He's speaking so fast that a guy from the next table frowns our way. Mason breaks off midsentence and we dive for our drinks, sucking at the straws and stealing a sideways glance at the guy. It's not long before he gets busy with his glass of tea again.

'But you understand now?' I ask when the coast is clear. *Are we okay?*

He pulls away from the coffee and swallows. 'Well, I understand why you couldn't answer all my questions.' His focus drops to the frosty glass in front of him and for a few seconds he doesn't speak. 'It doesn't explain why you won't jump with me, though.' The words come cautiously, almost bruised.

'I know.' I take my time, choosing the right words. 'It's just ... I've never been able to control my return. I have no idea how to train myself the way you have, and I guess I was scared.

What's stopping me from jumping ahead a zillion years? Ending up alone again?'

Now that I've been time skipping for real, I doubt that could happen. It's hard enough pushing forwards as far as a minute. But still, I find it a scary thought. What if one of us skipped ahead hundreds of years by accident? Or forgot how to return altogether?

'Scout.' His forehead is tight, eyes fixed on me. 'It's okay. I can help you. I'm getting better at it every day. If you learn how to control it, you won't have to worry about jumping too far.' One eyebrow lifts and stays there, and I find my shoulders relaxing.

For a while we're quiet, slurping the dregs of the coffees through our straws. Mason leans back and nudges my leg under the table with his knee. 'I won't ask you to jump with me until you're ready, okay?'

And I can't help grinning because he seems so sure again.

We spend the rest of the afternoon talking about the interval timers in our brain. According to Relative Time Theory, that's where we create our own time, so the first step is using it to measure our own sense of time.

'You don't have to time skip in between,' says Mason. 'Begin by working out the time from inside your own mind.'

'Okay,' I say, trying to sound confident.

'The first thing I tried is using my interval timer to wake myself up,' Mason says. 'What time does your alarm go off each morning?'

'Six thirty,' I say, thinking of Mum.

'Okay, so disable the timekeeper on your comscreen and tell yourself when to wake up. I bet you've already trained your interval timer, you just don't realise. And once you have the hang of that, try waking up at midnight, or one thirty or whatever. Yeah? You'll be amazed how quickly you get the hang of it.'

'So I just *tell* myself to wake up at six thirty?'

'Pretty much. Don't overthink it, okay? You're the one who taught me that.' Again, I feel his knee under the table. His mouth kinks up at one side and forms the cutest of dimples. 'Once you start using your interval timer, you'll learn how to use it when you time skip, yeah?'

'Yeah,' I say, adding silently, *I hope so.*

I can't disable the alarm. What if I sleep in and Mum's late for work? So instead I tell myself to wake at twenty past six. That way, she'll have no issue if I take a while to get the hang of it.

On the first morning I wake up at 6.28. Too easy. It's as if my brain was so used to the alarm that it knew exactly when to wake me up. It's not 6.20 but it's a good start. The following morning I wake up at 6.04. I'm getting the hang of this, sort of.

On the third morning I wake up just after five then spend the next hour and a half trying to get back to sleep. So of course when Mum's alarm sounds, I'm dead to the world. Fail.

On the fourth morning I wake every couple of hours, but somehow it gives me a sense of time passing and finally I wake up at 6.19. Nice. Except now I'm way tired and the next morning I sleep right through until the alarm.

Maybe my interval timer works better when I'm skipping through time. I've been practising skipping whenever I'm in our room alone. It's getting easier; each time makes me more confident I can do it again.

It's still so dark, so quiet, so *nothing* in the tunnel, but it doesn't send me cold the way it used to. Maybe because I know how to move through it now, only a few seconds for the first few tries, but now I can do closer to a minute a few times a day. By the time Mum comes home I've usually skipped forwards maybe four or five minutes in total. It's doing my head in a bit. Because when you think about it, I must be five minutes younger on those days than if I hadn't skipped.

It's crossed my mind that maybe I'm in no hurry to jump forwards a long way, because if Mason skips when I don't we'll end up that much closer in age. If he jumped ahead, say, two years, and I didn't skip at all, I'd be sixteen when he returned, the same age he is now. I'm two years younger than him at the moment, but maybe I won't always be. Weird.

My compad beeps late on Saturday morning. *Sorry to bother. It's Kessa. Want to meet up sometime? Maybe head to the park?*

It's like she's apologising for the invitation. If only she knew. I message straight back and we agree to meet later that day. We choose a park near the school, new territory for us both, maybe as a nod to our waiting future, even though it's still a couple of months until orientation day. And, as Kessa points out, getting there today is a dress rehearsal for when we're going every day.

We find a bench seat near the top of a rise, looking over a playground and a skate park. From here you can see the bits of land that used to be part of the park but are now high-rise flats.

The park is busy with citizens getting on with their lives. A maintenance truck trundles around, clearing away fallen branches. As Kessa and I chat, a couple of kids sneak over from the skate park and start teasing the safety sensors of the truck, standing so close that it triggers a change of path. I guess they must have done it before because they're really good at dodging and we get this sort of truck dance performance as it traces slow, wide circles to avoid the kids.

After a while the truck sounds a security warning, and the kids bolt with hoots of laughter. Kess steals a glance my way as the kids run off, pausing mid-sentence to check my reaction. It's almost as if she's asking for permission to find it funny. Of course, I'm doing the same thing, so we end up sharing a chuckle that gets bigger as we let go.

We finally calm the giggles and she picks up the conversation again. She's telling me about her twin, Malena, who only made it into a tech school. She's hoping for a transportation apprenticeship.

'She wants to travel, see a bit of the country.' Kessa sighs. 'So I guess it makes sense …'

Transportation workers only make D-grade rations at best. Maybe it's because they're twins, but it seems sort of harsh to have their lives mapped out so differently already. Kessa's set to make at least B-grade if she plays her cards right.

'So how is she about you making it into Karoly High?' I ask cautiously.

'Yeah. She's okay. Pretty good, I think. I mean, she would have sat the test if she thought she had a chance, but we all have to do what we can, don't we? Use the skills that we have to contribute.'

It's straight out of a textbook or a political speech. I'm not sure what to say.

'So you'll take the emergency stream if they want you to?' I ask.

'Yeah. If I'm better suited to that. Definitely if there are more jobs.'

'But don't you want to make your own decisions about your life?'

'Yeah, sure, I guess. But I'll take their advice if they give it.' She tilts her head towards me, a slight crease in her forehead. 'We're pretty lucky to make it into such a good school, don't you think? So we owe something back for the opportunity.'

She's textbook talking again. Her confidence in the system strikes me. Such unquestioning trust.

'So, what about you, Scout?' Kessa asks. 'Which junior school do you go to? I never understood why you didn't come to Footscray Primary.'

'Yeah …' I lift one arm and flick at some invisible insect. Brushing the idea away. 'I go to a school near Mum's work. It was easier that way.'

'Of course.' She nods meaningfully, trying to show that she understands. Although, of course, she doesn't. 'Cos she's … is she … is it just you both?'

She must have been dying to ask that question for years. 'Yeah, Dad's …' I pause. 'He's not with us anymore.'

It's sort of true.

Kessa places a hand on my shoulder while I guide the conversation back to her. Changing the subject fast.

I can't tell her the whole truth, at least definitely not until I get to know her better. And even then, I'm not sure it would be fair to dump her with that sort of thing. Once I tell her, she won't have the choice not to know.

For the rest of the afternoon I steer away from certain topics by asking Kessa more questions about herself. Safe stuff. I'll have to be careful if we're going to hang out together. All she has to do is add up a few key facts, and my whole world could fall apart.

'Ready?'

'Just one minute, yeah?' I'm sitting next to the whiteboard in Mason's garage, legs tucked to one side. A light blue blanket lies ready in front of me.

Mason must be kneeling rather than sitting cross-legged

like he usually does. His head and shoulders are visible. The comscreen is on the coffee table in front of us, the stopwatch running. We won't have anyone to hit start like we did when Mason was the only one jumping, so we're using the two-minute mark as zero.

The digits spin up to 1.45 and keep racing.

'Okay. Let's do this,' from Mason. The stopwatch reaches 02.00, and I hear a faint breath beside me.

My eyes close, shoulders relax and I exhale. Let myself sink. It's different with someone else here, harder to let go of my connection to the world around me.

Especially since that someone is Mason.

It takes longer than usual to still my thoughts and allow my sense of time to slow, but soon I find myself deep inside timelessness, a familiar place that's also foreign. My senses are mute as I drift forwards.

It's a safe amount of time, one minute. I pull up to the surface and gasp with the rush of it: the weight of my body against the floor, the truth of my own heartbeat. After being shut down in the tunnel, each sense is deliciously alive.

I turn to find Mason watching me. Our eyes meet but I don't say anything because it's hard to find words while I'm still being hit with here and now. He's breathing hard too, his face open and amazed.

'You saw me come back?' I realise it's the first time he's seen it. Still breathless. I have to find my brain somewhere in this flood of sensations. I reach forwards for the blanket.

His eyes follow as I pull it awkwardly around my shoulders, then drop once in a nod.

With two soft corners held to my chest, I shuffle around so that I'm facing him and lift a hand to rest on the whiteboard. 'Amazing, hey?'

'Better than amazing.' There's a pause as he keeps watching me but then he blinks as if making a decision. He shuffles in a quarter turn and places a hand, firm and warm, on top of mine.

We're here, his expression seems to say. *Real and okay.*

We don't need to speak, because I know. You crave any sort of contact after the buzz, confirmation that you're back.

He hasn't reached for his blanket but the screen shields him from my view. I can see the even skin of his chest and shoulders but nothing lower.

'I forgot to check the stopwatch,' I say as I remember. We both turn to the comscreen but it's pointless by now because already it's flown past 6.45.

Our hands haven't moved. He's already watching me when I turn back. 'Did you see how long you were gone?' I ask.

'About one minute and five seconds.'

'And me?'

'One thirty, I think.'

I let out a sigh. 'So I was late.'

'Maybe not. How long did it take before you went in?'

'Don't know.' But I see what he means. 'A while, I think. Maybe as much as thirty seconds.'

'You did it, though,' he says. 'Jumped with someone else here. Even though you weren't sure you could.'

'So did you.' I shift my position, but my hand stays in place. I don't think I could move it if I wanted to.

'Did you get any sense of me in there? With you?' asks Mason.

Head shaking. 'No. Did you?'

The drop of each corner of his mouth shows the answer: no.

I tug my thumb free and hook it over his. 'I don't think we even *exist* when we're in there,' I try. 'So how could we sense someone else?'

'We exist, I think,' Mason says. His eyes drift to my thumb. 'But we're part of everything, you know? That's how I think of it. There's no difference between you and me.' He looks up. 'No separation.'

Strange, but I know what he means. Until I knew how to skip it wouldn't have made sense to me. But now I feel the truth of it without being able to explain why, that sense of being everywhere and nowhere at once, both insignificant and limitless.

His hand doesn't move but I sense a change about him. 'Again?' he asks.

'Now? But I … I'm not ready.'

'We can wait if you want.' His hand drops but his face is still open.

'I'm not even sure I –'

'*Scout*. Don't stress. It's okay.' He cuts me off with a grin. 'We have all the time in the universe.'

CHAPTER ELEVEN

I'M UP AT six on the morning of Mum's birthday, my head too full of plans to sleep in. The extras from last night's delivery are stashed in a cupboard so I lift them onto the bench and quietly get mixing: flour, real egg and milk, plus a dash of vanilla. The batter waits on the bench while I dress and set up the breakfast tray.

The second pancake is ready to flip when Mum's alarm sounds. There's not much movement from the bed, so I wait for her to wake to the sizzles and aromas of her birthday breakfast. She's barely moved, but her eyes crinkle in a smile as I carry it all over.

'Oh … sweetheart.' Mum sits up, rubbing her cheek as I pat the doona flat and position the tray in place.

'Happy birthday, Mum!' She's warm with sleep as I lean in for a hug.

'This is lovely, Scout. Thank you.'

Mum's quiet as she takes it all in: two pancakes and a jug of real maple syrup on the side. I tried to get strawberries too, but that line was flagged 'unavailable'. Sliced lab banana had to do. Her present is carefully placed on the side of the tray, wrapped in pale blue tissue paper from the recycle shop.

As I watch, her head lifts to check out the bench and the bottle of maple syrup left there – the expensive stuff, of course – but she doesn't need to worry because I bought it with my credits, not hers.

She looks back at the present, and then up at me: 'So, um … what first?'

'Whatever you like, Mum. It's your day.'

Her answer turns into a yawn, but at least she seems pleased with the spread.

'Or have a shower first, if you like? I could keep the pancakes warm.'

A short pause, then: 'Actually, that would be lovely.'

'Okay, here.' I hold out the envelope with my chip in it. 'Swipe with this, and use all the hot water you like.'

'Oh, Scout. No, I can swipe for my own shower.' She collects her pants and shirt from the back of a chair but I step between her and the door, waving the envelope seductively in the air.

'Come on, it's my shout. You don't have to swipe for anything today.'

'Sweetheart, no.' I can tell from the creases on her forehead that I'm not going to win this one. Other than following her to the shower and beating her to the sensor, there's not much I can do, so I let her go and retrieve the pancakes, stashing them in the mini-oven to keep warm.

Two more rest at the top of the stack when she comes back, hair wet and pulled back in a bun. She seems crisper now, her lines in better focus than when she was fuzzy with sleep.

We sit with the tray between us on the bed, eating from the same plate like we used to when I was little. It gives me the tiniest twang about how it felt to share her food when we were so hungry. Maybe this is only one compared to thousands of meals, but at least it's one closer to paying her back.

I eat my second pancake rolled in one hand while brewing her a cup of tea, sweetened with a teaspoon of honey as a treat. I carry the steaming mug over to her, licking the last traces of maple syrup from my fingers.

She blows on the tea, places it on her bedside table and checks the clock. Still twenty minutes before she has to leave and anyway, how could they be angry with her for turning up a little bit late on her birthday?

'Come on.' I hold out the present.

She unwraps carefully, gently pulling off the tape to be saved for another day. Inside is a big box with two layers of homemade chocolates, a mix of soft centres and hard.

Her eyes go wide and she bites a lip, pulled tight from her smile. 'Yum. Thank you.' She doesn't look quite as happy as I thought she would, but I'll chalk it up to surprise.

'That's just the start.' I pick up the itinerary and unfold it for her, a whole weekend of fun and indulgence already booked:

a Spanish movie at the cinema this evening, then tomorrow afternoon a full hair treatment before dinner with her two best friends.

Her mouth shapes some of the words as she reads down, her eyes growing larger with each item and her eyebrows drawing closer. She reaches the end and looks up, confused.

I act as if I haven't noticed. 'What do you think? A whole birthday weekend of indulgence …'

Her focus drops as she reads aloud from the list. '2.15pm, hair treatment at the Riphair Salon?'

'Yeah, you deserve to be spoiled.'

Her confusion barely shifts. 'But a hair treatment? Scout … you realise how much those things cost?' She shakes her head.

'It's a present. You don't need to pay, I've already booked you in.'

'But we can't afford anything like that,' Mum keeps going. 'When have you ever seen me go to a *hair* salon?' Still, she doesn't get it.

'But that's the point. You would have been able to save up for this sort of stuff if not …' I wave my hands around to complete the sentence. *If not for me.* 'So now I have my own credits, I'm paying you back. A little bit, at least.'

It's only the slightest shift, a kind of fading in her face until she's staring across at me through a fog. She's meant to be happy.

'It's a present, okay? So you have to accept it.' My hands rest on my hips as I add, *'And* enjoy it.' There. She's been told.

Still she just stares at me so I pick up the tray, carrying it back to the kitchenette while she stays on the bed.

'Better get ready for work,' I call over my shoulder.

I'm sponging stickiness from the plate when I feel her hands on my shoulders.

'Scout, you don't have to pay me back.' Gently Mum tugs, trying to turn me around. I stay where I am. 'You owe me nothing, understand?'

'But I *want* to –'

'Listen.'

'Just this once.'

'Scout, *listen*.'

This time when she tugs on my shoulders, I turn slowly.

'I went to see Dr Ryan the other day.' A slow sigh. 'The one who signed the termination papers when I was pregnant?' Mum's voice goes softer as she speaks, as if the words are difficult for her, even now.

'He's agreed to insert the chip, and use the new fading procedure for the scar. We can trust him, more or less. But … his price.' Mum inhales slowly. 'He's asking for a hundred thousand credits.'

'*What?*'

'I know. He's risking more this time around, and I suppose … he's not stupid. And what are we going to do? Go shopping for a lower bribe?'

I lean backwards against the bench, all my plans slipping away. Her birthday dinner, the hair treatment …

'We need to save every credit we can from now on. I'm sorry, I should have told you already.' Her face brightens, maybe a little too much. 'But hey, why waste credits on a haircut, hey? It's just going to grow back.'

She chuckles at her own joke, but I'm not ready to join in yet. So many credits, just to fade a stupid scar.

'But maybe ...' I choose my words carefully. 'Maybe there's no reason to pay the bribe. I've been fine without it in my wrist so far.'

She's trying to understand, I can tell, but she has no idea. 'Scout, you're going to Karoly High School! So from now on, you'll need to think, act ... *look* like a citizen.'

'Yes, but I'm doing that already. I even managed my first ever friend link.' I could keep going, but I don't. I never would have made it back to my cave that time if I were stuck with the chip in my wrist. The more I think about this, the more I think it would be useful to be able to drop off the grid every now and then.

'Listen,' Mum slides an arm around my waist, stepping beside me, 'we don't have to book in with Dr Ryan straight away. All I'm saying is that we should save our credits. And even if we don't need them for the bribe, then we might ...' As she inhales, there's a slight catch in the flow, '... we might need them for other reasons.'

She has plans that she's not giving away, I can tell. A new place to live, maybe. A hundred thousand credits could go a long way. But I decide not to push it for now. 'Okay.'

We still go out for the movie that night, but it's not quite the mood I was aiming for. Throughout the whole evening Mum keeps fading into a sort of fog, forcing her expression to lift whenever she sees me watching.

It's only when Mum's about to wave off the lamp later that night that she finally says, 'Thanks, by the way. The hair treatment? It was a thoughtful gift.'

I finger the corner of the doona, not looking at her. It's not going to be a gift anymore.

The bed rocks gently as Mum rolls my way. 'Stop thinking about paying me back. I'm your mum, Coutlyn. And you're my daughter. Some things only work in one direction.'

Like time travel, perhaps, I want to say, but don't.

She reaches out and her hand brushes my shoulder before pulling back. 'I had a choice, okay? And I'd do it again in a flash. But it was my choice, not yours. You had no choice. The sacrifices I've made are not your fault, okay?'

She doesn't wait for me to say anything, just waves the lamp off and snuggles in.

I turn mine off too, but I don't sleep for a while. That phrase keeps going over and over in my mind. *You had no choice.*

It's after four on a Friday when I rest my bike in the shade against the garage wall. It's so stinking hot that I feel like the rubber of the tyres might go soft and sticky. The back of my shirt is wet when I pull off my backpack so I stay in the shade and suck down half my water bottle before gulping for breath. I end up with a noseful of thick, sweet air from a honeysuckle bush growing near the door.

It's been hot every day of the two weeks since my first jump with Mason. We can return within seconds of each other now. I haven't told Mason that I can't jump any further than a minute, but it doesn't seem to matter. And anyway, I'm in no hurry for longer jumps. The further ahead he goes when I don't, the closer we become in age.

I'm able to drop into the tunnel faster now, too. It takes only a few seconds for me to sink, but I'm nowhere near as fast as Mason. He can do it in the space of a breath; just closes his eyes, and he's gone.

He's getting more accurate with his time away, and already I can feel him moving on. That's how it works with Mason, I've realised. He obsesses about a goal as if nothing else in the world exists but the instant he achieves it, he moves on to the next.

We haven't spoken about it openly, but I think I can pick the next obsession. If I'm right, it's the ultimate goal, the reason behind all the others.

The side door to his garage is slightly open when I knock. No answer comes, so I knock again. Wait some more. He's letting all the heat in.

'Mason?' I slide the door further open and stick my head in, enjoying a breeze from the air-con. The room's empty.

I'm three cautious steps inside, dumbly peering around, when Mason's shape appears from thin air in front of me.

'Boo!' he shouts, before stumbling sideways.

A gasp escapes with a squeak of surprise. One hand slaps over my mouth. It's just Mason messing around. He managed to jump and land from standing – way impressive – but I'm not about to cheer him for it.

Mason's shoulders jiggle with laughter. 'Gotcha, didn't I?'

I breathe out, head shaking. 'Just you wait, I'll get you back.' Pretty sure I must be bright red, and not just because of the heat. I grab the blanket from the floor and throw it at him as hard as I can. He catches it easily and wraps it around his waist, grinning madly at me the whole time.

Something causes the door to move and a gust of hot air makes us turn.

'Heeee-ey.' It's Boc, his one word starting out high but then dropping in tone when he sees me.

'Hey,' Mason and I say at the same time, but our words come rushed and it suddenly feels as if we've been caught out.

'Hey, mate,' Mason says again, grabbing his shorts from the couch. I get the sense that he's adjusting, shifting in a way that he doesn't need to when I'm around.

Boc crosses his arms. 'Been skipping again?' Beads of sweat stand out on his hairline.

'Yeah, heaps.' Mason gestures my way as he steps out from behind the couch, shorts thankfully on now. 'And Scout too.'

At that, Boc's eyes move to me and stay there as if taking me in for the first time. It makes me want to look away but I force myself to meet his gaze.

'You've been time skipping too?' His eyes narrow thoughtfully.

'Yeah, sometimes.' My eyes drop without my permission, so I bring them up again.

He seems confused. 'Really?'

I'm not sure what else to say. I hug my arms against my chest.

'Anyway,' Boc turns back to Mason, 'I was going to ask if you want to come climbing with me and Amon again?'

Mason glances at me. 'Bit hot.'

'There's a cool change due tonight. We're meeting tomorrow at two.' Boc lets his arms drop. 'Training at the climbing centre, and then drinks at the end.'

A shrug from Mason. He doesn't seem overly keen. 'Sure. I guess.'

'Come on, Mase. Forget about last time. You just need some practice.'

'Is that all? Co-ordination might come in handy too.' Mason laughs.

Boc's face changes completely as he grins, and finally the room loses some tension. I swipe the back of my neck with a hand. I'm still sort of sweaty even though it's cooler inside.

'Okay. Good.' Mason says finally. 'Want to join us now?'

For some reason it feels strange with Boc here. I'm wondering if I should go, but Boc shakes his head. 'Nah. Catch you.' A glance my way, and then he's through the door with another gust of hot air.

A waft of honeysuckle lingers after the door closes behind him.

'Did he go because of me?' I ask after a moment of silence.

'Nah,' Mason says, but he doesn't sound convincing. I can't help thinking that Boc could have called or sent a message to ask Mason about climbing. It's as if he dropped round to hang, then changed his mind.

'Want a drink?'

'Nah, thanks.' One hand pushes into my backpack and finds the smooth shape of the water bottle. I pull it out.

'Come on. That must be five hundred degrees.'

Head shaking. 'I'm okay.'

Already Mason's swiping the fridgepad, pulling out two cans. I get this rich blast of coolness before he shuts the door.

'Here, try this.' He holds out a can. 'Bet you've never tried sherbet blast? It was all the rage last year.'

Again my head shakes but it's slower this time, more cautious, because I'm getting the feeling that he really wants me to take it; he's not just being polite. And he's right, I've never tried sherbet blast. But not because I was time skipping when it was released. We've just never had credits for fads like that.

Mason lifts my hand and makes a point of wrapping my fingers and palm around it. It's so cold that droplets of moisture are already forming on the outside. I look from the can in my hand up to Mason's face.

My shoulder lifts in apology because I'm still not sure what to do. When you see couples sharing rations, that's when you know it's serious, intimate. Like sharing blood, or something.

'Do this.' He holds up his can as if it's a demo model and

cracks it open. 'And then do this.' He takes a sip, swallows and lets out an *ahhh*. 'It's not that difficult, Scout.'

'I didn't swipe.'

'You don't have to.' It's with a tinge of impatience.

What a strange sensation this is, as if it's happening to someone else. I fumble with the catch as I crack it open, turning it into a joke. 'Like this?'

Mason's mouth forms a pout, assessing my technique. 'Very good. And now …'

As he takes another sip, I do the same. Immediately I get this explosion of fizz. My eyes go wide with shock as Mason cracks up.

'Good, huh?'

'Mmm.' My eyes are watering but I'm grinning too. We drop our arms at the same time and beam at each other.

He's still watching as I take my final sip, when — *tsst* — everything goes black and suddenly it's eerily quiet.

Mason swears under his breath as my eyes adjust to the only light filtering through the high window. The electricity has cut out.

CHAPTER TWELVE

'You okay?' Mason asks, just an outline in the dim light of his garage.

'Yep.'

'Juice better not be out all night.'

It's only when his compad sounds that I realise his parents mustn't be home. Mason's busy promising that he's all right when my compad beeps.

'Where are you?' Mum asks as soon as I answer.

'I'm fine. At Mason's.'

'They're saying it's almost the whole city.'

'Fantastic.'

'Might take them a while to fix this one, so I want you to stay put. Okay?'

Smartcars still work, of course, but they can't recharge, so taxis get overbooked and take hours – if you're lucky enough to get one. Plus, the backup generator for the public transport system has a habit of breaking down every time they have to use it.

Some people died from heat exhaustion a year ago when their train broke down in the underground loop.

'I have my bike —'

'No way. I don't want you out at all, understand? Bad things happen when there's a blackout. Can I speak to Mason's mum or dad?'

'They're not here.'

'Ask them to call me when they get in?'

'Okay.'

It takes a few more rounds before she signs off, so when I hit disconnect Mason's already finished.

'All okay?' I ask. Already the burn of outside is threatening to seep in.

'Yeah.' Slowly he breathes out. 'This is going to suck.' He reaches for the fridgepad and does a test swipe. Of course, nothing happens. 'Can't believe there's still no backup for the ration sensors.'

Mason collects torches from upstairs and positions them around the room. Then he starts pacing restlessly, a leopard trying to think his way out of a cage.

The whole ration system shuts down whenever the power cuts out, even water rations. Especially water, actually. Their security locks are so tight that there's no way around it without power so whenever there's a blackout, the stress levels in the city rise like heat off the pavement.

A couple of years back, most of the northern suburbs went without water for three whole days. Nearly a quarter of the city's population was forced to move in with friends and family. They sent out these huge water trucks with armed guards for the people who had nowhere else to stay. The whole city went totally stir crazy, there were twice as many car accidents because tempers were so frayed. The Richardsons had their daughter and son-in-law move in with them, just one room for four people.

So after the water came back on, there were these big rallies campaigning for changes to the ration swipers, an override system in an emergency. The government funded an inquiry that took eight months to reach the conclusion that the security risk is too great to set up a secondary access system. What if it meant that illegals were able to hack in? So of course everything stayed the same as it's always been.

'Listen.' I stand up, hands on hips.

Mason keeps going. On his next trip past, I have to stop myself from grabbing his shoulders. *It's okay,* I want to tell him. *I can get water without the sensors working.*

Though, of course, I can't tell him that.

'Why don't we skip ahead?' I try. It's only just occurred to me.

Mason stops. 'Now?'

'Sure.' The idea takes hold. 'Think of it as a test. Like, see how we go skipping in all conditions. Maybe we should be doing it in other ways too, like when it's really noisy or something.'

'Yeah.' He wet his lips before pushing them together. 'Or cold. Make sure you can jump in all conditions ...'

'Exactly.'

I suggest we don't skip too far in case Mason's parents come home before he's back, but really it's because I still haven't jumped further than a minute. Soon we have the screen set up and blankets ready.

For once I think I'm the one who drops away first, enjoying the peace that comes from the tunnel after the heat of the garage.

The return is like how it feels when you leave a movie, re-entering the real world after the cocoon-like bubble of the theatre. The heat hasn't seeped in yet, but even so the air feels thicker. Heavier.

Mason comes back about thirty seconds after me, sweating but calmer, too. In finding a place where his time slowed, his mind must have slowed as well.

'Okay?' I ask over the screen.

Mason drops his chin, still breathing hard. 'Again?'

I nod.

'Hang on.' We've skipped our way through so many minutes that it's already dark when I realise that the walls aren't pressing in quite so much. We pull on our tops and shorts before leaving the privacy of the screen.

The door won't swipe open without electricity so I do a manual override. The lock disengages and I push sideways to open it as I'm greeted with the most exquisite waft of cool.

We're both outside in an instant, arms up and spinning in the fresh air. A double flash of lightning brings everything into view before it drops away again.

Mason grabs my hand. 'Come on.'

He's heading back into the garage when I pull back. 'In here again?'

'Trust me.'

The heat is thick as he leads me through the garage and up the stairs to the main part of the house. We keep going up to the second level and into the master bedroom. Sort of weird, but before I ask where we're going, Mason leads me out onto a small balcony and the cool of outside.

Heat escapes from the brick walls in waves. I don't dare look down, heights not being my strong point, but before I can say anything, Mason drops my hand and grips the rail of a metal ladder leading up the wall to the roof. He clangs his way up until he disappears over the top ledge.

All I can do is follow, my hands slippery with sweat and my heart pounding. I almost fall over the lip that rims the flat roof and I land on hands and knees.

Mason's in the centre of the roof, looking out over the thousands of houses around this one. There's enough emergency lighting dotted around to make out the blocked skyline of the city to the east.

'Look.' As Mason points, a dash of lightning brings the city into focus before dropping away.

I find my feet and make my way over to him.

'Haven't been up here for ages,' he says under his breath.

My eyes adjust as we stand and watch the show. There's a stillness about him making me hesitate to speak.

'The last time I was up here was with my brother,' Mason says eventually. 'Storm breaking over the city …'

I wait for him to keep going, but he stays quiet so I ask, 'Where is he now?'

'Somewhere in Myanmar. Probably gone.' The words come slowly, difficult to get out. 'Missing in action.'

I give it some time, then prompt again. 'And … he's why you want to go backwards in time?'

In the pale light he shakes his head. 'It's not possible, I know.' But from the way he says it, I know I'm right. This has been his goal all along.

'What would you say?' I ask. 'If you could see him again, I mean.'

In the dim light I see Mason push his lips together, holding the emotion down as he stares out over the city skyline. 'I'd tell him to flunk out of uni. Take the art course that he always wanted to do instead of medicine.'

I don't have to ask for more. They taught his brother to save lives then sent him to die in some other country's war.

A flash from the west makes us turn and wait until the thunder reaches us.

'I know what you're thinking,' Mason says quietly. 'If I ever learn how to travel backwards, then why haven't I come back and told myself how to do it?'

I lift one shoulder in a shrug, not sure what to say.

'I've checked on the grid. Didn't find any double-ups of my chip.' As Mason keeps talking, he sinks to sit cross-legged and

I do the same, shutting away the outside world behind the rim of the roof.

'But wouldn't you just ... I don't know, *speak* to yourself?'

'Maybe. I don't know.' His tone drops as he presses a finger into the spongy rubber of the rooftop. 'I had this idea, right, that maybe it's harder for your mind to cope with travelling backwards. So maybe you come back but you end up with amnesia or something. I don't know ... but I've done some hospital checks, just in case.'

'And?'

A sigh. 'And nothing.'

For some reason, the image of Mason hacking into medical records, trawling through patient lists for broken, fragile versions of himself, makes my heart catch.

Because what if he found himself, stuck in a hospital ward somewhere with no idea who he was? Would it help him discover the secret to travelling backwards in time? Or would the sight of his future self, confused and broken, block him from learning to travel backwards for fear of what he would become?

Something about my expression makes Mason rest a hand on my knee. 'It's okay, Scout. I'm okay.'

'We don't know it's *im*possible, at least,' I try. 'So that's a start, isn't it?'

'Yeah.' But his tone drops at the end.

'I mean, until it started happening I never would have imagined that human beings could just ... slip into another time. It's like ...' My head shakes at the wonder of it. '... so *amazing*.

So who knows what else we could learn? For all we know it's just the limitations of our minds that stop us doing heaps of stuff. Unless we can first imagine what might be possible, how will we even know to try?'

It's only when I break off that I realise Mason's been staring at me so intently that it takes him a while to pull out of the spell. He catches me watching and turns away so quickly that it's suddenly weird, awkward. I bite my lip.

Mason clears his throat and shifts his legs to one side. He leans backwards on one hand and points with the other. 'First star.'

The rumblings to the west have died down, but at least the air is still cool. Only the most precious of storms bring rain these days. Faint glimmers of light have appeared above us and to the east.

'Not the first,' I say, and point to another star. 'There. And there too.'

'Come on.' Mason lies backwards and pats the roof beside him. I lie back next to him, our shoulders close but not touching as we stare up into space.

'And there,' I say again, finding another one. 'And there.'

'All right, all right.' There's a smile in his voice.

It's almost as peaceful as the tunnel here, staring up into a sky that never ends. If I needed a reminder that the universe is infinitely more mysterious than I can comprehend, here it is.

'You realise we're looking backwards in time?' Mason says beside me. His voice is soft at the wonder of it. 'That little glimmer of light that we're looking at now,' he lifts an arm to point, 'first left its sun millions of years ago and has been travelling light-years across the universe to reach us here, now. For all we know, that star died long ago. We won't know until millions of years after the last of the light leaves it.'

I don't turn my head; my mouth lifts at the corners. 'Time-travelling starlight?'

'Sort of. Though it's more that each speck of light exists in all of time. It just depends where in the universe you are when you see it. Every moment exists at once, yeah?'

'Fair enough.' Though it's with a shrug of sorts because the stuff he's saying is hard to hold onto, the truth always just out of my reach. 'So … where do they end up?' I ask slowly. 'These specks of light. They just keep going to the edge of the universe?'

'We're not sure, really,' says Mason. 'They say the universe might fold back on itself. But who knows? Maybe the light just keeps travelling forever.'

We're quiet after that, thinking, or just being. I'm not sure I get it completely, but the idea comforts me: so many glimmering lights travelling through the universe, the never-ending lifespan of starlight.

'Scout?' Mason's voice is so close that it makes me turn. I find his eyes staring right back into mine. 'Jump with me. Now.' I've barely formed an answer when he keeps going: 'Don't think about it. Just jump.'

'Okay.' It comes out as a breath.

Together, we close our eyes. Instead of sinking, tonight I allow myself to lift, the focal point of my mind rising into the space above me. I'm both here and there, everywhere and nowhere all at once, feeling my way through space and time.

It's easy to feel my way out. I pull up with a gasp, my heart pounding and cool air against my skin as I turn my head to find that I'm alone, a shirt and shorts resting beside me.

He returns the next instant. His eyes open and fall on me. We're both panting hard, the truth of the moment building because this time is different. We synchronised our return without planning it, but that's only part of what this is about.

He rolls towards me and stops with his mouth so close that we're breathing the same air, connected by our body heat. I'm inside his warmth.

The next thing I know he touches his lips against mine. It's the softest of questions. We pull back at the same time and when our eyes meet there's no question anymore. We fall together again, closer and surer. He holds firm as I press forwards, dizzy with the way it feels to have him so close.

Soon I have to make myself pull back to inhale slowly because otherwise I think I might forget to breathe. A shared smile, and then we're joined again, skin to skin. How strange to have been on my own all my life and now find myself here, with him.

I'm not sure how long it is before we part, separate but still together. Mason settles beside me again, head in one hand and his shoulder pale in the dim light. I roll onto my side and hook a foot over his bare leg. Our eyes stay locked the whole time.

It's only when the city whirrs back to life that we leave our rooftop cocoon.

———————

Mason sends a message on Monday afternoon. *Hey, you free to come over?*

Who would have thought that a small bunch of words could zing me such happiness? I wasn't expecting to see him until next weekend.

The bike ride gives me time to move through some nerves. Excited-nerves, but still. That night of the blackout we entered whole new territory, Mason and me, so I'm not sure what to expect from this afternoon. Can't wait to find out.

Boc's there when I arrive. I push aside my whiff of disappointment, smoothing my shirt down after the ride. He must have known that Mason asked me over, so the fact that he stayed can only be a good sign.

'Hey. How was the climb yesterday?' I ask him.

'Yeah, everyone was pretty wrecked after the blackout. So we only went to the climbing centre.' Boc jerks his head towards Mason. 'But we got Mase here to climb the high wall. No harness.'

My eyes pop. 'No harness?'

Mason shakes his head. 'I had a harness on, just didn't use it.'

'Next time,' says Boc. 'There's always next time.'

We all go quiet as Boc slaps his hands, rubbing the palms together. 'Well. That's it for me. Catch you later?'

Mason replies as some sort of look passes between them and it makes me wonder how much Boc knows about the night of the blackout. He seems better about me being here today, at least.

When he jerks his head my way, I search for words to say. *You don't have to go because of me.* Or something like that. But I can't think of anything that wouldn't sound weird.

Neither Mason nor I speak at first after the door slides shut behind Boc.

I mush my lips together uncomfortably. 'So ...' But I'm too slow because already Mason has turned away and is busy at the comscreen.

'Want to jump?' he asks, eyes on the screen.

'Sure.'

Mason sets up the whiteboard without another word, dropping the blanket on my side, just like always. It's as if the night of the blackout never even happened.

Mason goes to sit on his side, but I stay where I am.

'You okay?' I ask. Because so much has changed for me, but everything he's said and done so far is as if nothing has changed for him.

For the first time since I arrived, Mason stops to consider me properly and I know my eyes are full of questions. *What's going on?*

'It's okay, Scout. Just jump first. We can talk later, okay?' He says it with kindness, but it somehow makes me feel young. Silly. As if I'm dumb to have thought that our kiss meant something.

So I push my lips together and lift my head. Trying to show that I'm okay about it all. I can be cool about these things too. With legs crossed I take my place beside him, the whiteboard between us. 'One minute?'

His eyes lower. 'One minute.'

I draw in some air and shut out the room. My focus is all about getting to the other side of this skip. Maybe it will be good for us, a way of connecting again.

It's peaceful inside the tunnel, the absence of all worries.

When I pull out, my breathing comes fast. I'll never grow tired of that rush. Only a minute has passed and yet we've entered a whole new time.

Mason's not back and a change of atmosphere hits me straight away. I'm not sure how I pick it up but there's a clear difference between then and now. I catch a whiff of honeysuckle in the air that I'm sure wasn't there before.

When the seconds continue past and Mason still hasn't returned I peek over the screen to find nothing there, not even clothes.

My heart skips hard, faster now as I fumble beneath me for my clothes, leaving the blanket untouched. None of this feels right.

If something went wrong with Mason …

Underwear, shorts and singlet on. My shirt isn't here. This is so *not* right. I'm crawling in a desperate circle when I sense movement from behind the coffee table.

'Looking for this?' A figure stands from behind the comscreen.

It's Boc, holding my shirt. From the hardness in his face, I see in an instant.

He knows what he's holding, hidden in a pocket seam.

Beside him is Mason. In the seconds it takes him to stand and turn to me, I'm hit with a slap of truth.

Mason's been here all along. He let me skip on my own so they could watch what happened on the grid.

They know.

CHAPTER THIRTEEN

IT'S BOC WHO says it. 'You're not chipped, are you? It's hidden in your shirt.'

My head shakes, but no words come. What can I say? They would have watched me disappear while the chip stayed in full view on the grid.

Mason steps from behind the comscreen and stops beside me. One hand rests against my shoulder blade before falling away. 'You were born before they started chipping babies, way back in the 2020s. That's why it's not in your wrist.' He pauses and gestures towards Boc. 'Tell him, Scout.'

When Mason turns back to me it's with such certainty, such trust that my heart lifts and wedges in my throat. He's waiting for me to say that all is okay, what happened between us was real, I'm still the person he thought I was.

But, of course, I can't.

It's hard to even meet his gaze and, strangely, Boc is the one I turn to now, maybe because he has already guessed the truth. He's watching me calmly, patiently. But I see victory there too.

Boc's eyebrows lift in question, but all I can do is shake my head. *Please don't make me say it.*

'Admit it. You're illegal,' says Boc.

His eyes track across to Mason and narrow in a way that makes me think they've been arguing about this. But somehow that's even worse: Mason would have been defending stuff that doesn't add up because that was easier for him to contemplate than the idea of me being illegal.

'Scout?' Mason whispers.

I can't even look at him. What could I say to make any of this okay?

All I can think is that the reason they were able to find me in the first place is in Boc's hand. And that it's also the only way the police would be able to track me now.

And that gives me an idea.

A single wipe of my palms against the sides of my jeans, and I make a dash for the door.

Boc's closer than me and reacts with crocodile speed, blocking my way. His chest is pushed forwards, filling the space about him. *No you don't.*

I spin back to Mason for help, but this time his face shadows and he turns away.

No wonder. Trying to escape was as good as admitting who I am. Boc crosses his arms and I realise there's no way out.

The answer is there, on the grid, and hidden in the shirt in his hand. Nothing I can say would explain any of this.

Nothing except the truth.

'I found a woman at Footscray Park.' My voice is weak but I push through, and keep going. Just keep going. 'It was the night she returned from the two-year jump. She was sick ... dying. I wanted to go for help, but she stopped me.' A pause. 'I was with her when she died.'

I'm looking at Boc but my attention is on Mason as I speak, sensing his reaction as he realises where this is going, feeling the space between us grow as he steps back behind the comscreen.

When I've finished telling the whole story, Boc says, 'So ... you never knew how to time skip? You learnt ...'

'... because of you.' But of course, I'm speaking to Mason. And now that it's out, a wave of frustration comes behind, rising as hot tears that I wipe with my palm.

In the silence that follows, I find some small hope and slowly lift my eyes to Mason. He's staring at the space just in front of me, as if trying to make sense of my words, searching for a way to reconcile them with who he thought I was.

Without looking at me, he moves towards Boc and mutters something I don't catch, their heads bowed together. I don't have to hear it to know what they must be talking about. They have decisions to make: what to do about all this; whether to turn me in.

It's enough to absorb their attention, just for a moment. So I take my chances, making for the door to the main house and doing a manual override as I hear a cry of surprise from Boc behind me. The catch disengages as I hear the end of Mason's reply. ' … her go.'

In seconds I'm up the stairs and out the front door, headed straight for my bike. I'm barely in the seat before I'm pedalling down the driveway.

Leaving the chip behind.

The city streets blur with tears.

I wipe them with the back of my hand only to find that I'm also blinded by rage. It grows with each push of a pedal. How could I be so stupid? I was trying so hard to prove I knew how to time skip that I didn't think what the chip not being in my wrist could mean to anyone watching on the grid.

And now, everything's lost: my chance at school, a normal life. Food rations. Mason.

Can't think about Mason. My head fills with other losses. Kessa won't be able to message me anymore. And after all that she's risked for me, all that she's gone without, how am I going to tell Mum?

Mum.

I'm already halfway home when I realise my mistake. Still not thinking straight. I skid to a stop, turning back the way I came to take the Flemington path and soon I'm pedalling hard for the city, clear about where I have to be.

Use your head, Scout. There's no time to curl up and cry. Now more than ever I have to think my way out. I was speeding towards a place to hide, but I'm not the one who's in danger.

I'm already off-grid. I could survive on the water from my underground spring, maybe try growing food again to trade with illegals beyond the city limits. But even if I escape, the history map of that chip will always lead to our room. The minute I brought it home, I put her at risk of being caught. The one in danger is Mum.

I think about messaging her with the compad but decide against it. Anything like that could be intercepted and read. By Mason and Boc. Definitely the police. My only advantage is keeping my next move off-grid.

When I make it to her work building I stash the bike but of course the doors won't open for me anymore. To the system I'm invisible again. It's such familiar territory that I fall back onto my old tricks like pulling on a worn old coat. I used to use them just to get by, now I need them to survive.

Patience. That's my way to make things happen. For twenty minutes I bide my time until I'm wandering nonchalantly past the entrance at the same time a delivery drone shows up and we just happen to go through the double doors together. I make it to reception in its wake then turn for the stairwell. I'm ready for a manual override but when I test the door I find it unlocked, swinging free with barely a push. Must be the fire escape, too.

She doesn't like me coming to work but I've done this before, turning up when I was so bored that Mum telling me off was a reasonable way to fill the day.

I climb two steps at a time, coming out again on the sixth floor, forgetting for a moment which way to turn and spinning a full circle before I remember.

She's alone in her office, tapping at the comscreen. I slide the door shut as soon as I'm through, glad that her clients need privacy because now, more than ever, we do too.

'Coutlyn?' Annoyance is not far away, until she sees the state I'm in.

Mum is already with me as I crumble, still coming to understand what I've done. I thought it was my risk to take; didn't think about the risk for her.

'What happened?' She holds my shoulders, crouching beneath my bowed head. I'm too ashamed to say it but I have to because the police might be coming for her. 'Something's happened?'

I nod through the tears, but there's no time for crying. 'They ... they know. They have the —'

She cups her hand over my mouth. 'Shh. Don't say it.'

Mum leads me to a chair so that we're face to face but when she goes to lean away I grab her wrist. 'You have to dig it out. It's the only way.' It's the only way I can keep her safe.

'No.'

'We could live with the illegals, I could get water for us.'

'Coutlyn.' She untangles her hand from my grasp. 'No.'

'The grid is going to lead them to our room ... to *you*. You have to dig it out.'

'I said *no*.' It's sharper this time. Harder. She takes a breath. 'Tell me what happened. Quietly.'

At that, the tears slow. I'm suddenly numb inside.

'Mason and Boc,' I begin carefully because it's hard even to say the names. 'They know I'm illegal. They know I stole a chip.' The first would simply have me transported out of the city, but the second is way worse.

'And they're going to the police?'

'I don't know.' Even now that he knows the truth I can't believe Mason would do that to me. But Boc is another matter.

Mum glances at my singlet top, just briefly but long enough for me to see the way I'm dressed through her eyes. Normally I wouldn't go out like this; I'd throw a shirt on too. I twist away from her in the chair, arms shielding my stomach. It's not what she's thinking. Although in some ways, it is.

Mum leans back, closing her eyes as she rubs her temples. 'So they have the chip.'

I pull out the compad, hack into the grid and zoom in to Mason's house. I've never done this in front of Mum before but she leans forwards to watch without speaking.

There's no-one in Mason's garage but when I pull up to the rest of the house I find two dots in Mason's room. Him and Boc, I think at first. Then I recognise only one is tagged from when they followed me, and my breath catches. My shirt. He must have taken it up to his room.

I have to clear the lump in my throat when I see that, although I'm not sure if it's with hope or because of what I've lost.

Mason's not the one who most scares me, though, so I track back to when I was last at the garage, find Boc and follow where he went since I left. He stayed with Mason for about half an hour, and then went home.

'No contact with the police, from what I can find,' I say, scanning quickly through their recent activity in another window. But for how long?

'Okay. Let me think.' Mum stands and tests the lock on the door before turning my way. 'So we don't know for sure that they'll say anything.'

I shake my head, more at the frustration than agreement. 'But if they do —'

'Then we'll deal with it.' A pause. 'I could have run away to live with illegals once before,' she says evenly. 'But I've chosen a different path. I'm not living without a chip unless I have to. Now more than ever we're going to need the rations, the credits. Okay?'

No. Not okay at all. 'So … what? We just wait for them to come and arrest you?'

'No. We wait and make plans. We use our heads.' She drags her chair closer to mine and sits, our knees almost touching. 'But most of all, we don't do anything stupid.'

It's late by the time we leave her office, walking side by side through the entrance doors so it's not obvious she's the one who triggered it open. It's such familiar territory that there's no need to talk about it.

Mum catches the train home just like always but of course I ride my bike, stopping every fifteen minutes to check her progress on the grid, making sure she's still travelling in the right direction, towards home.

We spent the past two hours thinking our way ahead of the police, sorting out our stories, playing around with the what-ifs. Places to hide. A meeting place in case we're separated.

If the police investigate, there's a lot they won't understand. The history map of the chip is going to confuse them no end, but we can use that to distance Mum from all this. I am an illegal who was born outside the city limits, so our story goes. Mum found me living at the park and offered me a place to sleep. There's no proof that she knew the chip was stolen and no proof that I was living with her before the chip showed up. The fact that she's a social worker fits in perfectly, unless they're smart enough to run DNA tests. Maybe she'll get away with a slap on the wrist, I've begun to hope.

Maybe I'm the one who's most in danger after all.

I could get out of the city for a while, until we know whether Mason and Boc will turn me in, but I'm not leaving Mum alone.

And anyway, I'm coming to realise that I might have a fighting chance if they find me, even without all of the plans I've made with Mum. Because I can be here, and then not.

Time skipping might help me escape.

CHAPTER FOURTEEN

M UM'S HOME BEFORE me, of course, and two potatoes are already peeled and bubbling in a pot. We work in silence, naturally cutting back the portion sizes to only what's needed. Neither of us is hungry, anyway.

We watch a sitcom without taking any of it in, grateful that the movement and sound on the screen make up for our silence. Even though it's late, I doubt either of us will sleep.

It's a bit after eleven when Mum mutes the comscreen and I hear the front door engage. No idea how she picked that up. In silence we wait, listening for clues. Alistair normally comes home around now, but what if it's not him?

A shadow passes our door; neither of us breathes as we watch.

It's only when we hear Alistair's door engage that we exhale. No-one has come for us. Not yet.

Mum's eyes travel back to the comscreen, drawn by the flickering lights. She doesn't seem to have noticed that we can't hear what's being said.

I can't help imagining what would be happening now if that wasn't Alistair who just walked in. What if it *was* the police?

The program ends and Mum shifts in her seat, tired but nowhere near bed.

I shuffle forwards so that I'm perched on the edge of the armchair, and turn to face her. 'Listen, there's something else that you need to know.'

She sighs, almost as if she was expecting this.

As I search for the right words, she tilts her head in a way that suggests she thinks I'm going to talk about Mason; how I came to lose my shirt. Maybe that's why I need to tell her. But that's not the only reason.

I've decided that she needs to know what's going on. She needs to know what I can do in case I need to do it in a hurry. Better for her to hear it from me now than to see something she doesn't understand later, in the heat of the moment.

'So. This is going to be a lot to take in. Just listen, okay? Hear me out.' A flick to switch the comscreen over, then navigate to the grid. I'm not sure if there's any need for a smokescreen, but I make sure it's been triggered. I've made a big enough mistake already, the worst thing I could do is add to the list.

'This is how they worked me out.' I bring up Mason at his house and go quiet while I check for any police contact. None.

I keep going. 'So that's Mason during the blackout last week.' I point. 'And that's … me. At least … the chip.' Her head tilts enough for me to continue. 'So then … around seven …'

I don't try to find words; just show her the moment when Mason disappeared.

All she does is drop her chin, still listening, because of course she could never predict what she's about to hear.

'So my chip stayed behind because it's not in my wrist.' As I turn back to the grid my eyes fix onto the dot left behind while I time skipped. I'm not ready for the way it hits me: so many emotions, so raw, so close. I can almost smell the whiff of honeysuckle. The trust that grew from skipping together courses through me, the learning and growing ...

My eyes close against the memory. Regret is a luxury I can't afford.

It's only when I turn to Mum that I'm able to focus again. 'Maybe I should show you,' I mumble.

'All right.' She's growing impatient, I can tell.

I slip off the armchair and cross my legs on the floor. 'So this is about the way time works. It's hard to explain, but ... once you learn how we exist within time, you can ...' I take a breath. *Just say it.* 'Travel through it.'

Her mouth scrunches, sceptical, as if this information tastes strange. It's hard to swallow.

Maybe it's cruel, what I'm about to do, but it's the only way to prove it to her.

'So, what you're about to see, it will be hard to take in, okay? But I promise, no matter what happens, I'm fine. I'm coming back. You just have to wait a few seconds. I've done this heaps already. It's perfectly safe.'

Barely a blink from Mum, as if I'm speaking a different language.

'I'm fine, okay?' I say it again to make sure that she can hold that truth while I'm gone.

Mum responds with a circular kind of nod, no idea what I'm saying but willing to go along with it if that helps bring this to an end.

I take a breath, close my eyes.

It's not easy finding the tunnel; something is holding me back. Can't watch out for Mum while I'm gone.

My eyes have only been closed for a few seconds when I have to give up. Failed attempt. It's hard doing this knowing I'm leaving Mum behind.

'Well?' She lifts one arm, tired and impatient. *Don't you think we've been through enough?* her expression says.

I'm tired too, sick of myself perhaps. It's the relief of nothingness that helps me go back, the promise of the rush. I've decided to show her the truth, so I might as well get on with it.

Mum shuffles forwards in the armchair. One final whisper, 'Don't be scared.'

I let myself sink.

––––––––––

Mum's behind the armchair when I return, her hands gripping the backrest as if using it to shield her against the unknown.

'I'm okay. See? I'm back.' I move onto my knees as I speak,

enjoying the buzz as I collect my clothes. Only a couple of seconds but it was as good as ever. Man, did I need that.

'What ... what was ... what did you do?' Mum's voice is faint at first, rising with her confusion.

'I know. Amazing, right?' My eyebrows go up. 'It's all about the way time works —'

But before I can keep going Mum rushes towards me, and pulls me to stand. 'Let me see you.'

Her breath is hot in my face, the strength of her fear already stripping the rush away. 'Mum. I promise, I'm fine. It's all about the way we exist in time, it's perfectly —'

The next thing I know, she's holding me to her chest, patting up and down my back as if checking I'm whole again. She finishes with a hug, a real one, squeezing so tight. 'I thought I'd lost you.'

'Mum, I'm okay,' I say softly. She feels so small, so scared in my arms.

She was speaking over my shoulder but now she pulls away to focus on me properly. 'My goodness, Scout ...'

'It's okay, I promise.' Once she hears about the way it works she won't be so scared. 'So everyone thinks that time is steady, right? But it's not. We're the ones who control time.'

'Control *time*?' Her eyebrows pinch, as her chin pushes forwards in disbelief. 'Coutlyn, you can't possibly think ... This is ... like nothing —'

'But you just saw for yourself. It's totally safe.'

'*Safe?*'

'Mum, I know what I'm doing.'

'No.' It's just a whisper at first, but then she says it louder: 'No. You can't know that, Scout. Not for sure. My goodness, what were you thinking? I don't want you doing that again, okay?' She peers close, searching my face for agreement. 'Do you hear me? I want you to promise.'

'I …' I shake my head. She doesn't need to be scared. Why can't she understand that? 'You could learn how –'

'Coutlyn!' As if I'm a naughty child.

'Fine! Okay! I promise!' I spit it out like the sulky child she's treating me as.

'Where did you learn that?'

'Mason.' I spin away angrily. I never should have showed her. She doesn't understand, can't see what an advantage this could be.

She's quiet as I lie on my side of the bed, curl away from her. Alistair would have heard our raised voices. Maybe even the Richardsons.

I'm not sure what she does next, but I lie here and try to block out her sounds, toying with the idea of skipping again. My heart is so tired. I feel the mattress rock as she slips between the covers on her side. I'm on top, trapping them tight, but I don't move to make it easier for her. There's an invisible line stretching between us. I roll the other way.

She clicks off the lamp, but there's no way I'm about to sleep. I know she made me promise, but it's a promise that I won't be able to keep.

Mum heads out before I'm up the next morning.

I'm still lying in bed when she comes home a few hours later, saying something about a doctor's certificate. No reason to move. If the police are coming, it won't matter if I'm dressed or not.

She glances at the kitchenette as she comes in, but says nothing about the delivery bag still sitting there. From where I'm lying I can see that she ate nothing for breakfast.

Of course, I'll do the same. We both know how this game works. She's had the same idea once before: that she can cope with almost nothing so that I have enough. My response last time was to match her food intake exactly, so that's what I'll do now. If she eats nothing, I'll do that too.

Mum sits on the end of the bed. She's managed to get a doctor's certificate so she can take three whole days off work. I'm not sure what she had to say to have it approved; you have to be the walking dead to get one of those things. She's not even expected to work via distance monitor.

'How are you feeling?' she asks once she's finished dodging my questions about how she got the doctor's certificate.

'Fine.' Although now I wish I wasn't lolling round in bed. Maybe she thinks that time skipping is bad for your health.

Her eyebrows flicker. 'I thought I'd lost you.' She glances away and her face tightens.

'I'm okay, Mum.' My plans to stay angry melt in an instant.

I sit up to hug her, my arms trapping her shoulders and my head resting on the back of her neck.

She squeezes my arms in response and we stay that way for a while. Soon she loosens them slightly. 'Mason taught you how to do that?'

I nod with my head against her back. 'Sort of.'

'And he can do it too?'

'Yep. It's safe, Mum.'

She doesn't say anything, but I feel a shift in weight as she changes her grip on my arms. 'And you could ... do it again?'

More nodding.

'If the police come?' She's thought of it too.

'Think so. I'll have to practise.'

Again she says nothing so I'm not sure whether that means she agrees it's a good idea. I decide not to push it. I'm thinking about asking if she wants to learn to do it herself when she speaks again.

'Have you eaten?'

I pull out from the hug. 'Not yet.'

Even though we don't say it, breakfast becomes a truce of sorts. We still have spare food around, anyway, the legacy of two whole rations. Our issue is how it's going to be a week from now. The ration points are still saved on the chip, of course. But without the chip to swipe for them, they're as good as useless.

After breakfast Mum starts packing in case we have to leave in a hurry: two backpacks holding a weird combination of survival tools and precious mementos.

Boc and Mason are at school when I check, exactly where they're meant to be. I should be glad, I guess, but I'm not. Seeing them there, living their lives, gives me a weird mix of anger and envy. I hate the power they have over me now.

Don't want to spend my life watching them on the grid. So I spend the rest of the afternoon writing a bot that will sound an alert if they go anywhere near the police. It can do the watching, so I won't have to.

_____

On the morning that Mum's due back at work, I'm sitting up in bed, watching her get ready.

'Just one day, and then the weekend,' she says as she's collecting her bag. She comes to sit on the bed. 'So far, so good, eh?'

'Yeah.'

'Call me at lunchtime, okay?' Mum kisses me on the forehead and heads out the door.

I can tell that she's glad to be going back. Who wouldn't be? We've spent the last three days waiting, watching, preparing, but we can't keep living like that forever. Time to get living again.

As soon as the door engages, I'm hit with the emptiness of this room, the blankness of the future stretching before me.

Don't want to think about it. I go back to sleep.

It's late morning by the time I realise there's no chance I'll sleep any longer.

I don't want to eat anything if I can help it. I'm wondering how to fill my time without expending too much energy, when it hits me that I know what I can do instead. After all, I wouldn't need food if I wasn't here.

Numbly, I find my place on the floor. Let myself sink.

I'll have to stay away longer than one minute if I'm to use this as an escape from the police, but it's not as simple as I thought. The longer I stay away, the harder it is to find my way back. It's scary here, like swimming away from the certainty of land as the ocean floor drops away beneath me. The future horizon seems so far ahead that I'm sure I'll never reach it.

I pull up to the surface and gasp, my throat choked at the hit of reality. I glance at the clock and see that I made nearly five minutes. The rush wakes me up; I'm engaged in a way that I wasn't before. And I made it further than ever.

How long will I need if I'm to use this as an escape? Ten minutes? Half an hour? I have to keep practising, make sure.

I only need to prepare for a few minutes before I'm ready again. Once more, I sink.

The improvements have been slow. Even after weeks of practice, I'm barely able to jump ahead ten minutes at a time. Pushing it further always brings the unease of being anchorless; swimming into the endless ocean with no certainty I'll ever return.

I'm able to jump in quicker now, though. A breath, shoulders relax and I'm in. It's become my little routine, three steps to oblivion. And I've begun dropping away from different positions, too; on the bed at first and then perched on the edge of a chair.

I'm able to drop into the tunnel from just about anywhere these days, but the returns are taking practice. Once I lost my balance from sitting on the edge of the bed, and another time crumpled from the chair, ending up with a lump on my forehead. But I'm better at it now. As soon as I come back I'm ready to engage with the world, and can catch myself before I fall.

Lately I've begun to return from a skip, take a few breaths and then disappear into a fresh one. My days have become a wave of in and out, up and down, the calm of the tunnel and the rush of return. It's one way to pass the time, only living through part of it. And there are other benefits, too. I've found that I need to eat less. If I'm here for only half the day, I only need half as much. And besides, the energy after each return sparks my heart and wakes my mind.

The skipping has messed me around in other ways, though. Usually Mum heads for bed around nine thirty and I'm still wide awake at one in the morning. So one long night a couple of weeks back, I gave up on sleep and just skipped ahead through it, bouncing out and back again through ten-minute chunks of time. By the following night I was tired enough for bed. Since then I've begun to sleep only every second night.

I missed meeting Mum for lunch one day because I didn't realise it was Friday already. Another time I picked up a conversation I thought we'd left off earlier that day. It wasn't until Mum grimaced, searching back in her memory for the reference, that I realised the conversation must have happened days before.

Real time, or old time, or whatever you want to call it, isn't what it used to be. The more I skip, the less I'm contained by the normal cycles of life. Sunrise, sunset; day following night. I simply move through it all, skimming the surface like a separate and perfect drop of oil on an ocean of time.

Maybe it's because my skips are smoother these days, my chance to escape growing ever higher, but I've begun to feel less afraid too. Each day that passes has become one more day where Boc hasn't gone to the police; each hour that I'm free is one more hour that Mason hasn't turned me in.

It's weeks since they worked me out. Maybe they're going to keep my secret. Maybe, just maybe, I'm safe. And if that's the case, then everything's different. Because there's still a chip on the other side of the city, complete with my deets, clocking up energy rations. A tiny key to the future that I thought I'd lost.

But maybe I can steal it back.

CHAPTER FIFTEEN

First stop is the grid. I haven't checked it for ages – after writing the bot to keep an eye on Boc and Mason for me, I haven't needed to. Even after all this time I shift a little in my chair before going in. Don't want to be reminded of what it used to be like, can't think about the way they must see me now.

Just get the job done, Scout.

I set up the firewall, track across to the school and immediately find Mason. There he is, right now, sitting in class. Just a simple dot on a screen, but already I've fallen into it, my thoughts travelling back to how it used to be. The way it felt to be exploring a new kind of reality with him, discovering the truth of time travel together.

I have to get my head around the way things have changed, but I still don't know where I stand. What has he been thinking since I ran that day? How does he feel about me now?

My eyes close as I lean back and shake the thoughts away. Other questions are more pressing; some that at least can be answered.

It takes only a few seconds before I shuffle forwards in the chair, regaining focus, and take control again. I pull the grid back over the past weeks to see a long-term overview of where he's been, in case I missed anything that I should know about. It's pretty much what you'd expect: school and home, home and school with a restaurant on the weekends. Still no police visits and the chip is still in his room, same as it used to be. From what I can tell, it hasn't moved since I last saw it there.

The security system for his house is set up to trigger if any barriers are broken, just as you'd expect. But I can't find any other controllers on the system, so it must be wired into some sort of onsite com, I guess. I'll have to get closer in order to disable it.

Next I pick up Boc's dot from his house and check him the same way, a long-term overview of his movements these past weeks. I'm ready for a crazy scribble all over the city, here and there, meeting friends and heading out of town to go mountain biking, so I'm not prepared for how neat his worm is. Home, then school, then over to Mason's garage. On Saturday afternoons, he heads over to the indoor rock-climbing centre. That's it.

Strange. It doesn't seem like Boc at all. When I zoom out even further to check his movement over the past six months, my breathing grows more wary. Because his crazy scribble all over town continued right up until the evening he found me out.

Ever since then, he's stopped heading out of the city, stopped most of his climbing with the Spiderboys. You can clearly see a difference between his movements – his life – ever since that night. But why?

The unusualness of it makes my throat tighten and I have to walk away from the comscreen. *Think, Scout. Think.* What did I miss?

No idea. Back in I go, checking and double-checking for police contact, double-thinking what I haven't thought to check.

I should be glad, I guess, because in some ways he seems less of a loose cannon now. I bite my lip. He's more contained, more focused …

I'm zoomed out too far to catch any of the time skips, so I pull out of the grid and bring up Mason's garage in real time. It's easier to follow back from the present moment, so I start from today and track back to yesterday to find them: two dots, Mason and Boc, together on Sunday afternoon.

Once I have them in the garage I zoom in closer and track the worms back hour-by-hour, minute-by-minute.

Immediately, I find a gap in one worm. Boc must have been timing Mason, I guess.

The return time was at 5.14pm. Carefully, I track back the seconds until I've reached a full minute: still no dot to show the moment when Mason dropped off. Backwards again, five minutes, ten. Half an hour.

My heart pounds at the power of what this means. I've never seen Mason time skip for this long.

Back I go, further still, until I find his worm again. He disappeared at 3.51pm, which means he stayed away for eighty-three minutes.

Wow. I lean back in the chair, taking it in. Mason was able to skip nearly ten minutes the last time I saw him; but this is way new territory, well over an hour. I have to admit, I'm impressed. Maybe a speck jealous.

I should be planning how to get the chip back, but I'm curious. I'm at the moment on the history grid when he disappeared yesterday so I track backwards from there, checking to see if he jumped earlier in the day as well.

I'm tracking back minute by minute so that I can pick up the smaller time skips. At 2.45pm yesterday, I stop.

There's another gap, except …

My head tilts as I realise. This gap is in the *other* worm. It's only seven minutes but still unmistakably a gap. *Boc?*

Impressive, if it was one of his first.

Strange that he's in the exact same spot where Mason used to sit for his time skips.

Now that I think about it, the worm with the long jump was sitting on the couch. Mason never skipped from there when I was around. I realise that I'm not entirely certain that the first worm I tracked was actually Mason. I tagged them both when they first followed me but never added names, so I just assumed that the one jumping had to be him.

My hands move quickly, tracking back to a time when I can see for sure who is who. Mason would have been alone in his bedroom on Saturday night, so I tag that dot with his name.

I return to the dots yesterday afternoon, and my mouth falls open as I gape at the screen. I was right. Mason wasn't the one who jumped for so long. It was Boc.

If I can make it into Mason's house without triggering the alarm, I'll be able to get the chip back. I pick a day that Mason stays after school for band practice and his parents are both at work. Don't think I'll need that much time, but I head over as soon as it's safe in the morning. In and out, that's the plan.

Mason's bedroom is upstairs, so first I check out the fir tree growing outside his window. It only takes a minute of squinting into the sunlight to decide that the branches are way too thin to carry me. I'll definitely have to make my way in at the ground floor instead.

I find a place in the garden out of sight from the neighbours and start searching on my compad for the security system. The air is heavy and warm, even though I'm in the shade; the heat is thick with dust.

Now that I'm within the zone, it's easy to see what's going on. It's just a simple old electrical circuit set to trigger an alarm if any doors or windows are opened. I might be able to just cut the power, but there could be a backup battery that catches me out. Better to play it safe and disable it completely.

It's slow going, partly because I don't know what I'm doing and partly because I don't want to leave any traces that I've been messing around in here. Once I make it out with the chip I'll need to return the security system to the way it was. I work methodically, making sure I have a record of each change I make. Can't leave any dumb surprises that give me away.

It's about an hour before I'm ready to go in. The alarm even gives this little ping when it disengages, so I know for sure that all is clear.

Instead of working on the front entrance, I head around to the garage. It's hidden from the street, but it's also familiar territory, I guess. This almost used to be home.

It takes only a second to do a manual override.

I'm pushing the door open when three clear crunches of gravel sound behind me.

A sharp intake of air as I spin around, heart pounding.

It's Mason, in school uniform and just standing there, casual as anything. As if we'd organised to meet here in the middle of the day.

He crosses his arms. 'You took your time.'

I'm so unprepared that I actually let out this weird, awkward laugh. I have a strange flash of being happy to see him.

Mason doesn't smile back. 'I thought you'd come ages ago. You've been getting around stuff by hacking all your life, haven't you? That's why you're so good at it.'

I swallow. It wasn't a question. All I can do is stare down at the path between us as I find my way back to the place we are now. 'But how? I mean how did –'

'I set up an alert to tell me if someone was tampering with our security system. Figured it was only a matter of time.'

Of course. The program I found on the main grid must have been added by Mason.

No idea what to say, where to look. He's caught me out. I cling desperately to the knowledge that he could have called the police weeks ago. There must be some reason why he hasn't.

'Come on.' Not even a sideways glance as he strides past me, pushing the door open the rest of the way and continuing inside. When he reaches the opposite side of the room he stops to turn back my way. 'Seriously?'

I'm still here, barely inside the garage space, hovering nervously.

'If I was going to turn you in, don't you think I would have done it a long time ago?'

'I know. Sorry.' I shake my head.

Creases appear on his forehead before he turns to keep going.

Still, I don't move. I call after him: 'Why haven't you?' I have to know.

Mason stops but doesn't turn and I'm left staring at his back. His head turns so that his face is in profile. 'I don't know, Scout. No freaking idea.' The words come sharp. Hard.

Okay. So that's where we are.

Mason continues into the house, and this time I follow him

up the stairs to the main house, then up a second flight of stairs to the bedrooms.

When I make it to the doorway, Mason already has the shirt draped across both hands as if taking care not to wrinkle it.

He stretches his arms towards me, still refusing to meet my eye. As I step forwards and take the shirt I can't help smiling. 'Thank you. I mean … I can't tell you …' He's given me my life back.

Already I'm feeling for the slip of paper wrapped around the chip. Mason drops his arms and strides away from me, ending up beside the window, as far away from me as possible.

My fingertips find the familiar lump inside the paper and my whole being lets out a sigh. So good to have it back. And now that I have the chip I'm reminded once again of the woman. *I'll make it count for something,* I promised her once. I hope I can still make good on that promise.

Mason hasn't moved, one hand holding back the curtain as he stares out at nothing.

'So what now?' I ask.

A glance my way. 'What do you mean?'

'Well.' So many questions. What next with time skipping? *What about us?*

'Do I need to be worried?' I ask.

Back staring out the window. 'No.'

'What about Boc?'

Mason doesn't move. 'You don't have to worry about Boc.'

'You sure?'

'Scout, the minute anyone tracks that chip, they'll find the gaps in our history maps. We don't want to be answering questions any more than you do.'

He's right, of course. But I didn't realise until yesterday that Boc has gaps in his grid map as well.

I can't help going there. 'Boc jumped for eighty-three minutes? How did he manage that so soon?'

My reaction seems to help bring Mason out a little. 'Told you, the guy knows no fear.' Our eyes meet for the first time since he found me out and it almost hurts, being seen this way. I force myself to stare back. There's softness in there, deep down and hidden. He hasn't forgotten.

'How long can you stay away these days?' he asks.

'Nearly ten minutes.'

Mason goes quiet again, but the tension's eased. 'Have you tried to go further?'

'Yeah.' I shift my feet. 'But it's like I'm being held back or, I don't know, I'm scared I'll get lost if I go in too far.'

Mason doesn't reply, just clenches his jaw. He's quiet for a while and I expect him to ask more questions, because I have questions too. Has he found the same changes to his sleep patterns that I have? Does he find that he doesn't need so much food when he skips?

'Better get back to school,' he says, to the window.

At first I don't move. I'm not ready for it to be over.

He stays staring out the window, so I force myself to turn and make my way out of the room. I'm not expecting him to follow but when I head out and into the sun, I glance back to find him close behind.

He starts tinkering with the security system and I'm left hovering, wondering. The door shuts with a *shht*.

Mason turns my way, lifting a hand to shield his face from the glare. 'She's your mother, isn't she. Miya?'

I'm working out the best way to answer, the best way to protect her, when he snorts and lets out a dry laugh: 'You look totally alike.'

'Yes. But she never knew about the chip. That was all me.' No matter what else happens, I have to keep her safe.

It's as if he hasn't heard, staring into space and shaking his head. 'You know what really gets me? I had no idea. Never guessed once.' He shrugs. 'Stupid, hey?'

'Not stupid.' I take a breath. 'You just believed what you wanted to believe.'

'Tchyeah.' He's not just angry with me, he's angry with himself for not realising.

'Mason, that's just human nature –' How often do we hold onto an idea that we wish was real rather than face the truth?

He's not listening. 'And the woman? Did she say anything before she died?'

'She was barely conscious.'

'What about her deets? Did you see anything before you wiped the chip?'

I tear a strip of dry skin from my fingernail as I try to remember. 'I don't think they were real. Maybe time skipping messed around with the records.' There was nothing on there that you'd expect from an old woman and the insertion stamp was too recent to make any sense.

Mason pushes his hands into his pockets. 'I can't help thinking, if I'd *been* there when she came back. I knew what she was capable of doing, and I wasn't there. So many questions I could have asked. And now –'

He shakes his head, eyes narrowed. As if it's my fault.

I think I understand. Everything that happened between us, in Mason's mind, was meant to have been with someone else, a strange mash-up of that woman and me. A person who doesn't exist. The kiss, the synchronised time skipping, none of it would have happened if he knew who I really was.

Even though it smells stale and old, I slip on the shirt. This is the best way to keep it safe. The bike stand takes a second push with my foot before it clicks back.

'Thanks,' I mumble, and bite my lip. 'For not turning me in.'

No reaction.

Guess I wasn't expecting any. I swing my leg over the seat and roll towards the road, blinking away the tears.

CHAPTER SIXTEEN

THE MOOD IS one of stunned relief when I show Mum the chip. No celebration. We came too scarily close to a future without it.

The credits have been clocking up this whole time, but we're still thousands short of the hundred thousand we need to have the chip inserted. Mum goes to visit Dr Ryan anyway, asking if there's any way we could have the procedure done now and pay the rest back in instalments.

At least the answer isn't difficult to understand: Payment upfront only.

I'm disappointed when I hear that but it doesn't slow Mum. As soon as we hear back from Dr Ryan, Mum shifts to her plan B: a veterinarian willing to accept cases like us on the side. The vet is even more expensive than Dr Ryan, but she's willing to do the procedure straight away. It's just a matter of paying an extra fifteen thousand credits as interest. I almost refuse to go ahead with it when I hear that; she's taking advantage because she knows we're desperate.

But as Mum points out, we *are* desperate.

On a Sunday afternoon only a few days after I got the chip back, I find myself in a doctor's surgery in the city. No idea how a black market vet came to have access to this surgery. Of course, I don't ask.

The veterinarian is tiny, her shoulders so narrow that she reminds me of a child. At least, she would if she weren't so terrifying. Maybe it's the way she holds her mouth or the way she talks to the space just above my head, but sitting in that surgery begins to make me feel way more invisible than I've ever felt by being off-grid. If I do ever get caught and this insertion is traced back to her, I have no doubt that her blood pressure will stay completely steady as she tells the police she's never seen me in her life.

Most people would turn away, I guess, rather than watch their flesh being sliced open. But I find myself transfixed, sort of horrified at the blood and the thickness of white tendons, and also amazed at the difference between this and the first time I saw the chip.

It's only when I'm hit with the memory of cutting that woman's wrist open that I have to look away from the chip, trapped between titanium tweezers as it's lowered into my wrist.

How strange. That was the last time I'm ever going to see it. My flesh will grow around the chip just as it did for the woman who died. I'm not just using her credits now. From now on she's quite literally part of me.

We make an appointment to return in three weeks for the fading procedure once the wound has healed. Then I simply walk out of the surgery, a normal citizen whose wrist has been strapped because of a sprain. No need to look twice; nothing unusual here.

The doors slip open as I approach, no different from when I used to keep the chip tucked inside a pocket, but as I stride through, my steps feel stronger, bedded to the earth.

I'm really here, a citizen. I've arrived. The doors shut behind me automatically and I continue to the station, expecting an easy and safe train ride home just like everyone else. I'm happy and relieved but also keenly aware that I'm shackled in a way I've never been before. Everything is different now; there's no going off-grid anymore.

I conjure up my gratitude for everything that's been made possible by the piece of metal and plastic now residing in my wrist. The best news of all is that I made it just in time for orientation day.

Karoly High is a distance out of the city. I read somewhere that it was designed nearly ten years ago but you wouldn't know that from walking through the grounds. It's sleek and modern with triple-glazed windows everywhere. There's a huge oval with a running track around the outside, and although I know the grass is fake – it has to be – the colour seems so real and it sinks so naturally under my hand when I test it that it's hard to believe it's not real, live, water-guzzling grass like they have on display at the Botanic Gardens.

You can tell the kids who are here for orientation, not just from the way our uniforms are spotless and just slightly too big, but also from the way we all stick together, nervously shuffling along in packs.

After the initial tours, there's assembly and a pep talk from the principal. Then we're sorted into mentor groups. Kess is in mine, thankfully. I'm not sure what I would have done if we'd been separated; our shoulders have been as good as glued since we climbed on the train at Footscray this morning. I told her that I've been injured, that's why I've been out of contact, and she seemed to believe me. We've pretty much picked up from where we left off.

The mentor teachers take us through the timetable, study expectations and what to do if we hit any trouble. Then it's time to visit the specialist teachers. The science block is huge and broken into various departments: medicine, chemical engineering, nanotechnology. A whole corner of the school has been dedicated to crop beds of wheat and vegetables for testing bioengineering techniques. The further into the day we go, the more I keep thinking how amazing it is that I made it here. How close I came to having it taken away.

A bit before lunch break, I'm called in for a full medical

check-up, my biggest risk for the day. I've already prepared answers about the bandage on my wrist, even practising my *ouch* if it's touched. But the medic seems more interested in testing my fitness and metabolism than checking a sprain. She asks a bunch of questions about my sleep patterns so I give her answers based on the way I used to sleep. Before time skipping.

I've only just walked out of the med lab when there's a ping on my compad. A whole heap of files have landed in my school account: when I should go to bed; how much I should eat; times of day that I'll study best. So many resources focused on me being my best, one of the chosen ones, with the future of the nation resting on our shoulders.

Kessa catches me rubbing the back of my wrist during the lunch break, still tender after yesterday. I've already told her it's a sprain.

'You okay?' she asks, a loaded fork hovering. 'Is it hurting?'

'No, it's all right.' I grasp a can of water with my good hand and gulp.

'How did you do it?' she asks and takes a bite of spinach.

Carefully I place the can back on the table, swallow, and summon the words I've already prepared about tripping on a tree root.

Before I let them out though, I glance over at Kess and find her watching me so closely that the words evaporate and I'm left only with dry air against my tongue.

How long will I have to fake my answers like this for? My entire life?

A pool of tiredness rises in me and for a second, I let myself imagine how it would be if I dropped a hint, maybe something about a secret. I could start by talking about illegals or something. Test the waters, I guess.

Then I get a flash of the way Mason last stared past me, the distance in his expression, and my mouth shuts. I already have the answer to my question about how Kessa might react. I've known for years how real citizens think of illegals.

Kessa's watching me as she chews, waiting patiently. She's so open, so quick to trust, that before I realise what's happening my eyes brim and tears threaten to spill.

It happens so fast that all I can think to do is drop my gaze, saying the words in my mind that I can never say out loud: *I can't tell you what happened, because I have too much to lose.*

'Scout?' Kess leans close, her fork already on the plate and concern in her tone.

But already I'm pushing it back. 'I'm sorry, it's nothing. I just fell.'

'Don't be sorry,' she says softly, and for a moment I imagine that maybe she's guessed. Somehow. But then she says, 'It must be way painful, you look wrecked.'

I lift my head, brush my thoughts away. 'It's okay. I'm okay.'

She thinks it's because of the sprain. 'Should we find a med room? They'll have a nerve block or something.'

'No, no.' Back on track. Finding a smile is easier now.

'Really? You sure?'

'Yeah. I'm okay.'

Maybe I can never tell her who I once was, but that doesn't have to stop me from sharing the person I am now. A citizen, just like her.

———————

Mum's only just left the next morning when the doorbell buzzes. I'm on the compad in an instant, my hands on autopilot as they swipe straight for the grid. The police?

A second buzz has already sounded when I find two dots, both already tagged. Mason and Boc.

Yesterday's shirt is slung over a chair. I slip it on, still in my pyjama bottoms, and pause at the disengage button. In my mind I repeat a reassurance: if they were going to turn me in, they would have done it ages ago.

Okay. Holding my head high, I hit the door open.

As soon as I see them standing there I have to step back. Wish there was more of a buffer between us.

'Hey.' It's Boc who comes forward, hands on hips. 'Get dressed. We want to show you something.'

'Show me what?'

'You'll see.'

I don't move, questioning Mason with my eyes. *What's going on?* He jerks his chin forwards. 'It's okay, Scout.'

Okay. 'Give me a minute.'

They disappear and I'm left scrambling for clothes, pushing away tiny sparks of hope before any take hold. This was how

I hit trouble in the first place. I have to be smart about this, stay sharp.

I think about messaging Mum and decide against it; don't want her worrying any more than she has to. Instead I bring up the grid on the comscreen, complete with firewall and fake browsing bot. Then I set it to track me on the grid. If Mum comes home tonight and I'm not back, she'll find an instant view of where I am and who's with me.

It's a message to her, but only if it's needed. Here's hoping it's not.

Jeans, boots and shirt buttoned almost to the top. Ready to run if I need to.

I make my way out the main entrance doors and find them waiting near the front gate. Mason's standing a distance from Boc, and it makes me wonder what's been going on between them. They had the chance to turn me in and decided against it. That counts for something. Doesn't it?

I make a point of keeping my expression even. 'Okay. Where to?'

'Come on.' Already Boc's moving, arms swinging as he leads us along the street.

Mason falls into step beside me, his hands sunk deep in his pockets as he glares at the ground just ahead of our steps. They both move fast; I have to concentrate on keeping up.

'So where are we going?' I ask Mason.

'You'll see.' No pause, not even the slightest turn of his head.

I'm quiet after that. He's here, with me, but also not.

Judging from the path we take I guess we're headed for the train station. We take the bridge to Platform 2, trains out of the city. A train arrives only a few minutes later. There are more seats available than on the trains headed into the city. I haven't travelled in this direction ever before.

Mason and Boc stay near the doorway, leaning against the rails, silent. We can't really talk, I guess. Not about time skipping. Not about chips. After hovering nearby for a while, I give up and find a seat.

At one point a guy sitting next to me climbs off. The train rocks into acceleration then smooths out as it reaches top speed. Mason leaves his handrail and makes his way across the aisle to slip in next to me.

Another spark of hope rises and I have to push it back down. Hold my hands in my lap, contained and neat.

'What happened?' He raises his eyebrows meaningfully towards my wrist, still in its bandage.

'Just a sprain.' I lift my arm and inspect the fastening. Still secure. I can't help pushing at the bandage on top of the wound, the pain a reminder of who I am now.

'Really?' he scoffs.

'What else could it be?' I scrunch my nose to mean *think I'm going to talk about this in here?*

He gets it finally, 'Yeah. Sorry,' and finds the space in front of him again.

We stay that way for the rest of the trip, saying nothing.

We reach Seaholme Station and I make a mental note. Have

to keep a map in my mind of where we're going. The pace is slower this time, out of the station and along the main strip until we reach the high steel fence of a school. Kids are crowded into a bare earth quadrangle, using the little remaining space for fitness drills. This class looks like it streams into basic emergency services but part of the skill seems to be dodging all the other kids in there too.

A teacher keeps calling out, 'Chins up! Chests out! Not long until water break.'

It's only now that I think to ask: 'How come you two aren't at school?' They aren't even in uniform.

'Study week,' Mason says simply.

I bite at some dry skin on my lip; still no idea what we're doing here. Usually kids in the mainstream schools get steered into the manual jobs like food prep and cleaning, but I can't see what this has to do with me.

Boc is focused on his compad, checking a couple of kids in the quadrangle before frowning at the screen again. We're making our way along the length of the fence when Boc stops and his eyes narrow. 'Back this way.'

He strides past us, picking up the pace, but this time I decide to stick with him. Boc's the reason Mason found me out, but I can't let that get to me. It's safest if he doesn't think of me as the enemy. I have too much to lose.

'So, um ... congratulations,' I say. 'You've learnt to time skip? That's pretty cool. And you stayed away for over an hour. I'm impressed.'

He's walking a step or two ahead of me, and pauses to glance back. His chest seems to inflate in recognition.

'So how did you manage your first jump?'

'Dunno.' Hands still on hips, no warmth in his expression, but at least his pace has slowed a little. 'You taught yourself, didn't you? I mean,' he shrugs, and his top lip curls: 'if *you* can do it ...'

It takes a few seconds for me to realise what he means but when I do, I have to stop walking. *If an illegal can do it, then anyone can.*

What am I doing here? I'm about to turn for home when Boc looks down at his compad again, then points into the schoolyard. 'There.'

My last spark of pride is begging me to walk away, but curiosity works its way in. I've come this far. Mouth set straight, I turn slowly and track along the line of his outstretched arm.

It's a girl around my age, her arms heavy with a box that's about as big as she is. Dirty potatoes are piled so high in it that the lid won't close.

She's walking along the edge of the school grounds. We're on the footpath outside, following a short distance behind.

I turn to Boc and raise my eyebrows. 'And?' I've heard that school kids do food prep for restaurants in exchange for references. Sort of slave labour but with the chance of a job once you graduate.

Boc's waiting with the grid already on display. 'Here.'

I stop walking, and summon the final piece of patience I have left. I'm thinking that maybe she'll have no dot; that they've found another illegal and expect me to watch as she's caught. Or something like that. So I'm surprised to see a dot moving along the fence line in real time, the grid clearly matching reality.

'See?' Boc asks, and points to show that the dot has been tagged with a name.

'Jaclyn Hurstbridge,' I read obediently. We start following again, moving slowly as Boc swipes at his compad again, only glancing up now and then from his screen to check where he's stepping.

Soon Jaclyn drops out of view as she turns a corner. We're slower as we turn down the side street but I pick her out a short distance ahead. She must be heading to the food prep area.

I glance over at Mason. 'So who's Jaclyn Hurstbridge?'

'Here.' Boc holds out his compad again to show a list of names, none that I recognise. 'This is the list of applicants for next year's intake at Karoly High. Two hundred people were offered places, including you.'

As I keep watching he scrolls past names, slowing at mine – 93, which makes my eyebrows go up – before he continues down. It's a while before we reach Jaclyn Hurstbridge. Her name is listed beside the rank 201.

As soon as I see it I glance up. She's still within view but moving slower now, as if the weight of the potatoes is wearing her down.

'We're not going to turn you in, okay?' Mason says.

'That girl was ranked 201,' continues Boc. 'Because you got a place, she didn't.'

It's almost too much. For a moment I can't speak.

I'm not sure which is worse: the way Boc brought me out here to show me this, or the way Mason went along with it. My arms lift in helpless frustration. 'What do you want me to say?'

'Just thought you should see for yourself.' Boc crosses his arms, an air of satisfaction about him. Maybe he couldn't risk going to the police, but he'll never forget who I am.

It doesn't matter that I sat the test fair and square, doesn't even matter that I scored higher than Jaclyn. She's a citizen, and I am not. In their minds I'm accessing resources that were allocated to someone else.

Unfairness balls and burns inside me, but my body is still. I won't give them the satisfaction. I'm holding it back, for now.

Before I can stop myself, my gaze lifts once more to Jaclyn. She's still within view, just.

My heart slows as she moves further away, growing ever smaller. She doesn't realise what has happened. What I've done.

The life stretching before her is so different from mine. Again the injustice flares, but it's different this time, cold, somehow, and still. This is the first time I've been on the other side. Her choices have all shrunk; her job prospects will be limited because of this school. I've always wondered how it feels to be on the inside, what it's like to be one of the chosen ones.

My eyes drop. Now I know.

'Come on,' Mason turns to go. 'Let's get out of here.'

They know they've hit me hard. I can barely move with the weight of this.

Boc falls beside Mason and they begin along the path with their backs to me. I can tell that I'm expected to follow.

But I don't.

And I'm not going to either.

They've only gone a few steps when Mason turns my way again, waiting. I've been practising for a different kind of escape but this will do just fine. My eyes fix on him as I drop into the tunnel.

Anywhere but here.

There is peace inside the tunnel, but I'm already deep inside nothing when I realise my mistake. I've lost all control, dropping further than ever before, sinking so fast that I'm tumbling, spinning inside empty space.

No idea where I am. No sense of which way is up or down. It's not panic I feel but a shifting fog engulfing my mind, invading my thoughts.

Blindly, I search for a way forwards, struggling to remember. There's somewhere I need to be. The further I fall, the thicker this space becomes. It gets even darker, if that's possible.

A vague thought comes to me. I should be panicking. How strange that I'm not; all I feel is the bliss of ignorance. No real plan to find my way out.

Only a distant, dimming memory of who I am.

CHAPTER SEVENTEEN

Mum.

It's Mum who finally brings me back. Or rather, it's the idea of her coming home to find me gone that does it; the knowledge that I have to save her from the worry.

All is quiet, empty; I'm floating through nothing when I sense a pull, the faintest of pulses calling me. It's enough to follow, gradually, moving slowly at first and then accelerating towards a pinprick in time. I have to return before Mum gets home.

With a gasp, I break through the surface, immediately certain of when I've returned. It's the same day, late in the afternoon. I'll make it back home in time.

My mind is buzzing, the air cooler now than when I fell away. The change in atmosphere hits me in an instant. Last I knew it was late morning, but now I find myself surrounded by evening. How strange.

How beautiful.

Soft clothes crushed beneath my feet. I lift them up one by one and slip them on.

There are red drops on the ground. My wrist is bleeding.

'Six hours and twenty-three freaking minutes!' I jump at the sound of Boc's voice, turning to see him and Mason stretching stiffly, as if they were sitting on the nature strip all this time. 'That was amazing.'

As if through a glass wall, I watch them moving towards me, slowly recognising the memories of the morning. I'm light, safe inside the space of a heartbeat, but I know why I'm here, why I fell away so fast.

Adrenaline gives me courage. 'I almost didn't make it.'

Mason pauses. 'The sinkhole?' He's holding the bandage, his forehead creased. 'You had trouble coming back?'

All I can do is nod, pushing my lips together at the memory of where I was. The emptiness of it doesn't scare me so much as the way I almost forgot who I was.

'Your wrist.' Mason points at the short strip of a wound. Blood streaks down my hand in threads. 'Here.'

He holds out the bandage and I become a one-handed muddle, trying to wrap it around. It's only when a drop wets the fabric that I realise I'm crying. A delayed reaction, I think. What if I hadn't been able to make it back?

I keep my head tilted. Don't want Boc to see.

'Here,' Mason says again. But it's different this time, closer. He takes the tangle of bandage and unwraps my feeble attempt so he can start again. I hold my breath as I let him work, keeping my eyes wide because I know that if I blink the tears will fall and give me away.

Mason's finishing with the fastening when two tears finally land on my arm, but he doesn't flinch. He's not going to make this worse than it already is.

'I'm sorry, Scout,' he says softly. Just for me. 'Okay?' He leans in close to look at me. 'We shouldn't have brought you here.'

'I'm not freaking sorry. I'm impressed.' Boc is standing a short distance from us, hands on hips. 'Six whole hours. This is a major breakthrough. How did you get back?' The way his jaw muscles bulge makes me wonder if he's a little jealous.

I look to Mason for support. 'It was Mum ... I have to be back before she's home, or she'll worry. I think it worked like a deadline that helped me back. I don't know. The time she's due home was kind of like a magnet or something, pulling me out.'

Mason rubs the backs of his fingers against his jaw. 'Interesting. I've found that the further I jump, the harder it is to stay accurate with the return. But this is good. If we find something to use as a deadline, who knows how far we could go?'

'A full day as a start.' It's Boc, closer now. 'But we need more practice. You have to train with us.'

'Nah, mate.' At that, Mason strides away from me and whispers something to Boc that I don't catch.

'Nah, she'll be right,' says Boc. 'She can help. She has to meet Amon and Echo.'

'Who?' I ask.

'A couple of climbing buddies,' says Boc. 'Amon and ... his sister. They learnt to skip even quicker than Mase did.'

There's meaning in the way he said the word *sister*, but I don't try to work it out because other questions are more pressing. 'Hang on. They can time skip?'

'Yep. Fast learners, eh?' Boc grins as if he expects me to be jealous or something.

Why is it that everything seems to be a competition for him? *It's not,* I remind myself. 'Yeah. Really good.' If other people have learnt how to skip, I want to meet them.

The return journey is different from the trip out. Boc keeps asking about my jump today and I answer as best I can, pausing whenever someone else is close enough to hear. It's not until we're nearly at Footscray Station that Mason makes his way across the aisle to me.

He doesn't speak at first, just pushes his mouth to one side as he thinks about what to say. I get the feeling that he doesn't want me to meet the others. No way he can stop me, though.

'So if you're sure about coming next week, make sure you can drop away in an instant.' Mason clicks his fingers. 'Like that, yeah?'

A shrug from me. 'Okay.'

'And more importantly, you have to be able to stay away at least five minutes. No coming back early.'

'How come?'

A grin from Boc. 'You'll see.'

'I'm not mucking around here, Scout.' Mason's face is deadly serious. 'If you can't be confident of staying away long enough then you don't come.'

I'm not sure of anything anymore after falling in so fast today, not at all confident I can do any of the stuff he just said, but the idea of being left behind again, stuck on my own, is worse than being lost in the tunnel. I've spent all my life being separated, different from everyone else. Now I know how to time skip I want to be around others who can too. Even if two of them are Boc and Mason.

I hold my ground and adjust my grip on the rail. 'I'll be fine, Mason.'

He doesn't seem sure, but by now the train has slowed and the doors are opening. I step off the carriage and swivel back. 'See you next week.'

The doors meet between us and I'm left with the final image of Mason, his chin lowered and eyes locked on mine.

As soon as Mum leaves for work the next morning, I'm up and ready. Feet apart, standing beside the bed, I wipe my palms against my pyjama pants.

A twinge from my wrist makes me cup it with the other hand, checking the bandage for signs of blood. The wound split at the edge yesterday but it seems to be holding now.

Yesterday. It's only the briefest glint but before I can hold it back the memory expands and takes hold. That steady fog; the way it felt to forget. A mug left beside the sink catches my eye. Maybe I'll brew some tea first.

I settle into the routine of boiling water and stirring concentrate, checking out the news sites at the same time. Not yet ready for jumping again, I settle in front of the comscreen with the mug in one hand. This is how my life used to be, before the chip and before time skipping.

Before I changed the course of Jaclyn's life.

How is it fair that I have to carry this guilt?

Then again, how is it fair that she won't get the chances she could have?

I can't face the news at the moment, so I end up scrolling through online programming tutorials. I know most of them already, of course, but I haven't come here to learn. I'm here because these tutes are familiar and safe, like curling up in bed after a hard day. Just for a while I relive a time when my dreams were simple and clean.

For something to do I bring up a coding program and start tweaking some lines of script I've been playing with. I used to spend days trying out all sorts of weird program patches. Except, instead of little programs that made it easier living illegal in the city like I used to write, this one is a masking code to hide me from the grid.

It takes a few weird workarounds, but by mid-morning I get to the point when I run the program and my dot disappears from the grid.

For a while I just sit here, invisible and safe. This is the way life used to be. Except as soon as I move, the chip re-triggers and the dot re-appears. The script needs more work, but it's still good to know that it's there.

When I check the clock, I realise I've messed around for nearly two hours. Long enough. I switch off the comscreen and stand. My throat is dry but I swallow it away. Just let go.

I drop into the tunnel.

I'm away only a few seconds, the quickest of letting go before grabbing reality again. I make it back without any trouble, landing solid on two feet, my confidence returning with the rush of coming back.

Again.

This time I'm away a whole minute. Still no problem. It's good to be back in familiar territory. With each successful return, I feel more sure about staying away a full five minutes by next weekend. So I position my feet and drop into the tunnel again. Three clear minutes.

Then five. I've been here before, deep in the tunnel.

It's nearly midday by the time I break. Not much point in dressing, no-one to see me in here. I'm eating marmalade on toast when a possibility comes to me. There's still six hours at least before Mum comes home. And although five minutes is the minimum for next week's training, I'm sure Boc will be aiming for longer.

Draining a full glass of water, I finish and make a decision. The longer I leave it, the harder it will become. I've been there before, and made it out the other side.

I don't let myself fall in so quickly this time, don't plunge into nothing. This time I drop in neatly, carefully drifting from the anchor of now. I'm sure I can even sense my progress through time. One minute, now five, travelling ever further into an endless ocean, infinity domed above me.

So this is where the fear comes from, this sense of disappearing, becoming nothing. Or perhaps becoming one with everything.

The difference right now is that I still have a sense of where I'm from, a shoreline for return if I need. Already I can feel the pull of the evening, the promise of Mum returning home. I'm even clear enough to imagine resisting, continuing further past my curfew, but I don't. Not today.

It's nearly six when I pull up to the surface, gasping with the rush of the return and fresh with confidence. Knowing I could go further if I needed.

I'm finally pulling on clothes when I hear a message beep.

Saw you on the grid. Kudos. See you on Sat. M.

CHAPTER EIGHTEEN

O N SATURDAY AFTERNOON I ride out to the rock
climbing centre north of the city and somehow end up
taking the wrong path. I have to cut across town once I realise,
so I'm nearly twenty minutes late by the time I reach the blue
door at one side of the main climbing area.

Boc already warned me that it would be locked, so I send
him a message and wait. It's hot but that's not why my palms are
damp. Hope I'm ready for this. I've been jumping through the
long hours while Mum's at work, finding my way back every
time. But I know better than anyone how easy it is to get lost.

'Hey,' Boc whispers as the door edges open. 'We're warming
up.'

As he pulls the door, I slip through into a huge space and
immediately I'm hit with the focus in here, a calm concentration.
Mason is standing at the other end of the room, a whiteboard set
up beside him. Directly across from him is a guy I recognise from
the news story about Mason and Boc climbing the Macquarie

Bank building, and beyond him a girl of about eleven or twelve who has the same jet black hair and pale skin as the guy.

Along the length of the back area is a climbing wall covered in lumps and holes for supporting hands and feet. Three or four safety harnesses lie unused at the base.

'Scout. Amon. Echo.' That's the extent of the introductions from Boc.

'Hey,' says Amon with a jerk of his chin. 'You made six hours?' He seems so compact and strong, he reminds me of Japanese gymnast.

Small shake of the head. 'Just a fluke.'

'Don't sell yourself short.'

Echo has been staring this whole time, so I lift my eyebrows and try a 'hi'. She responds by pursing her lips and turning the other way. It makes me wonder how much Boc has already told them about me. Six hours time skipping. But what else? I can't help wondering how much I can trust them; more importantly, how much I can trust Boc.

'Okay. Let's do this.' Boc looks serious, but there's an under-current of excitement in his manner.

At his words, Amon lifts a yellow plastic gun and aims directly at Mason. His focus is along the length of the barrel, hands fisted and arms straight. It's only a toy, I think. But the way he's holding it makes me step back.

'What's going on?'

'Training,' Boc says, deadpan.

'On three,' from Amon, a statue.

Mason repositions his feet and breathes out. His shoulders relax.

The last time I saw him prepare was on the roof of his house, so long ago. There's a noticeable change about him. His eyes are steady, a clear confidence about them.

'One, two,' calls Echo, '... three.'

With a shot from Amon, the bullet tears through the space towards Mason. Only of course Mason's not there: he time skipped to avoid being hit. The bullet hits the opposite wall and falls harmlessly to the floor.

The silence is followed by a sucking gasp as Mason returns. I exhale, not because of the toy bullet, but because one day it could be real.

Mason grabs a shawl that was tangled on the floor and wraps it around his waist. 'Don't think we need the count in anymore. Maybe we can just say *one*?'

'Okay,' says Amon.

'Can I go?' from Echo. She steps forwards, hands behind her back.

There's a pause as Boc turns to consider her. 'Why don't you work with Scout?' he says.

There's no movement from Echo, but she has her back to me so I guess she said something I couldn't hear.

'No. What's the problem?' asks Boc.

'All right.' Her shoulders slump only slightly as she slinks away from Boc. Something gives me the feeling that I'm not the favourite training buddy.

Echo finds a second gun, glancing over at me here and there. She holds her mouth tight as we make our way to the other side of the whiteboard screen.

I take a cream knitted shawl out of my bag and set it up around where I'm standing so it'll be easy to pull around me when I return.

'Want to jump first, or shoot?' Echo asks once we're all set.

'You choose.'

Her eyebrows go up. 'I'll jump first?'

'Okay,' I say.

'Start with a count of three,' calls Amon.

It feels way wrong to start shooting someone I only just met. Haven't even seen her time skip, so I shoot at a nearby wall to test the bullets; they're just foam with a rubber tip. Even if I do hit her, she won't be badly hurt. But I know that even rubber bullets can bruise nastily, so there's definitely incentive to get out of their way.

Echo takes a few seconds to prepare, circling her shoulders, shifting her feet. Can't help glancing sideways as I wait. Mason's holding the other gun now. When he sees me watching he responds with a slight jerk of his chin.

'Okay,' Echo calls. 'Call *go*, and then shoot. Don't bother with a count of three.'

The others have been training on the other side of the whiteboard until now, but I feel them pause as I take aim. Echo shakes her head and shoulders, clearing the last of the cobwebs away.

I reposition my feet, and then call, 'Go.'

My shot travels left. I wouldn't have hit her, but it doesn't matter anyway. Echo isn't there anymore. Her clothes lie in a pile where she stood.

Silence.

Amon has stepped forwards to see around the screen. I'm sure he's been through this many times but even so, you still can't help that pause, the sense of anticipation. Everything on hold until you see that truth of a return.

It's been longer than the few seconds that Mason stayed away. I'm about to ask how many times she's done this when Echo's form takes shape above her clothes. She launches straight into a jump, her fist punching the air, her pale torso curving into a c-shape.

It's the strangest thing, nakedness. You can be standing here with no clothes and not feel exposed one bit. Not if you're focused on other things. Echo might have nothing on, but she's so comfortable that you almost don't notice.

Other times, you might have your clothes on but feel more naked than you ever have before.

'Yeehaa! That is brilliant, that is.' Echo takes a few steps towards me, grinning before she spins back for her clothes. She pulls them on frenetically, then bounces over to where the rest of us are standing. Time skipping seems to make that girl need to move.

'All right, let's do this for real,' says Boc.

Everyone else responds to that, packing stuff away and

carrying the harnesses into a store room. An air of calm focus still hangs about them, people with a job to do. I help with a harness when Amon asks but otherwise keep out of the way. Guess my turn's later, but I don't ask what's going on. Best to stay quiet until I know what we're doing.

Once everything's packed away we head out of the rock climbing centre and cut across to the back of the industrial estate. The sun's harsh by now, so we track a zigzag path between patches of shade.

Boc's been walking with Mason, leading the way, but when we reach an old fence he holds open a broken section for everyone to climb through, and ends up near the back.

'Thanks,' I say once I've ducked through.

No reply, but he falls into step with me. 'So one thing is bugging me,' he says evenly.

'Just one?'

'Mason reckons you taught him how to skip. How could you do that? You didn't even know how to yourself.'

I shrug. It's not as mysterious as he thinks. 'I hacked in to see stuff he was reading online, so I knew a bit about Relative Time Theory. That's all.'

I'm expecting that to be enough, but he slows as I step around a stinging nettle, sticking by my side. It's because he's stuck on me being illegal, I think. How could someone like me make any difference to anything?

'You really didn't know any more than that?'

'Well. I knew that it was possible. I learnt some stuff from looking at what happened on the grid. So I just used what I saw to make it seem like I could already time skip.'

'You would be used that, I guess. Making shit up?'

Anger flares in my stomach, but I push it away. *Don't take the bait.* Don't let him think of us as enemies.

But I have to say something. 'You know, we're not as different as you think,' I say evenly. The only reason he can't understand what I've done is that he's never had to fight for what he has. His whole life has just been handed to him because of who his parents are.

'Oh, no. We're different,' Boc shoots back straight away. 'Know why?'

I don't bother to reply.

'When that stuff started happening between you and Mase? If it had been me I would have trusted him. I wouldn't have kept lying about being illegal, I would have told him the truth. And if I couldn't trust him with the truth, then I wouldn't have been with him. You're so used to keeping secrets from everyone that you don't know when to stop.'

It's like a slap in the face. I can't help slowing a little, letting him stride ahead of me, even though it shows he's won. Maybe he's right. I'm so used to being illegal that I don't know how to think any other way.

We're making our way through open parkland by now, probably another reclaimed tip. Mostly dust, hardly any trees. I keep my eye out for clues about where we might be going. Shooting range, maybe? Public barbeques and picnic tables are dotted around, but judging by the layer of dust I don't think they've ever been touched.

The others have reached a fence at the other end of the park, overlooking three sets of railway tracks. Signs in faded red and black type decorate the length of the fence: *WARNING. No admittance. Trespassers will immediately be tagged. DANGER. Super-fast trains.*

Boc drops a backpack and frowns down at the tracks. 'When's the next one?'

'12.47.' Mason is looking down at his compad. 'The one after that's at ten past one.'

They must be freight, not passenger trains because I haven't seen this route on the grid. That means mega security and no drivers, just speeding machines carrying stuff from one side of the city to the other.

'Want to wait for the next one?' says Mason. 'You'll have time to warm up.'

'I'll make it.'

Already Boc's climbing the fence. I check the time: 12.32.

He makes it over easily, no alarm, no alerts triggered on the grid from what I can tell, and continues down the retaining slope towards the railway tracks, slipping once or twice on loose rocks.

'So … what?' I turn to Mason. 'He's going to stand on the tracks?'

'You can hear the train approaching,' Mason points to one side, 'about one and a half seconds before it passes.'

By now Boc has made it to the bottom of the slope and starts across scrubland towards the tracks.

'He has to stay away long enough for the carriages to pass through,' says Echo. By now she's perched on top of a wooden picnic table, as if settled in for some outdoor theatre. 'Those things go on forever.'

'Six hundred carriages,' Amon says. 'Sometimes more.'

I turn back to see Boc reach the first set of railway tracks and step over. 'Testing if he can jump under stress?'

'Yeah. You could say that,' from Mason. 'Simulating a danger scenario.'

'But if he doesn't jump in time, the safety sensors will trigger,' I say. 'And then what? He just has to bolt? Pretend that he was lost or something when they come after him?'

No answer. My eyes track across to Echo, who is busy picking at her fingernails. When I come back to Mason he won't meet my focus.

'What? You've disabled the safety sensors?' The accusation is clear in my voice. Boc might be asking for a lesson or ten, but this is insanity.

Mason places his hands on his hips. 'He asked me to do it. We can't be caught doing stuff like this.'

'Mason.' Head shaking. 'This is crazy. What if he panics?'

'He's ready.'

'But what if he isn't?'

'He'll be okay.'

'But –'

'Scout!' Mason stands away from the picnic table and strides towards me, stopping so close I can feel his breath on my cheek. 'His IP means he's going to military school next year, okay? Once he's been trained there's no refusing if he's called up. For all we know, the experience he gets today might just save his life.'

Echo swivels on the top of the picnic table. 'And Amon has the same IP.'

Not sure what to say. Amon just sits there, staring at his hands.

'12.45,' says Mason. It's too late for me to talk Boc out of this, even if I could scramble down in time.

We're quiet as we wait, Echo now standing at the fence with two fingers hooked in the wire above her head.

A high level hum is the first clue that it's approaching, followed by a series of flashes. Silver and white, with a blur of other colours. It all happened so fast that I didn't see if Boc jumped or not but he's not on the grid when I check.

In silence, we watch. Speaking might somehow break the focus, jinx Boc out too early. Or something like that. Echo's hand drops to wipe her palm on the side of her shorts then she hooks her fingers into the wire again.

Forever. That's how long the freight train takes, little more than a pulsing hum and a flash of light and dark.

Then, as suddenly as it arrived, the last carriage shoots out of sight and it's gone. All is silent.

Holding my breath, I check the grid to make sure that the dot I tagged for Boc still hasn't returned.

We're shifting cautiously when a lone figure appears on the tracks, his skin like dark silk in the sunlight. The whoop of victory says it all. 'Woohoooo!'

The other three let out cheers and applaud Boc as he pulls on his clothes and makes his way up the slope. Echo drops her head back while Mason raises his eyebrows at me. 'See?'

I shake my head, relieved, but not ready to celebrate.

Already Boc's climbing the fence to drop down on our side. He's breathing hard, full of nervous energy.

'That was freaking incredible.' Boc strides the length of the fence, his focus on the railway lines. 'You can feel these vibrations in the tracks so you know to be ready. But man, it was intense.'

'You knew how long to stay away?' I ask.

A pause, as if he's only now remembered that I'm here. 'Course.' A smug grin. 'Piece of piss.'

Now that I've seen him in action, it makes sense that Boc's skipping so easily. Scaling a city building, steering downhill on a mountain bike, jumping into the unknown: they're all about guts, really. No wonder he's able to travel so far. He's fearless.

'Who's next?' Boc clicks his tongue, tracking from one to the other until he stops on me. 'Scout?'

'Nah, mate, I'll go.' Mason moves forwards.

'I'm ready,' says Echo.

Shoulders square, I lift myself tall. 'I'll go.'

Mason steps beside me, his fingers cupping my elbow. 'No, Scout, wait until you've had more time to prepare.'

'I'm the only one who hasn't skipped today,' I say evenly. 'It's my turn.' None of them think I can do this; that's why I have to.

Before anyone else can speak, I wedge a boot into the fence. It rattles as I climb.

Just stay focused. Stay calm. Don't think about what might happen if something goes wrong.

I take smaller steps down the bank than Boc, slipping only once on a loose rock. I get to the edge of the tracks and check my compad. 1.03.

It's dry down here, dusty. Scrubland and tree skeletons. I find a place between the two tracks, their parallel lines stretching out before me. I look up and search along the ridge, easily finding the others lined along the fence, watching silently.

Check my compad. Two minutes to go.

Breathe out, allow my shoulders to ease. I'm tempted to jump now, get this over with. But the risk is even greater if I do that, I realise. If the train is late, jumping early might lead to returning too soon ...

Don't think. Just get to the other side.

Another breath and I sense a change in the atmosphere, a rumbling from the centre of the earth.

It's coming. I let out a gasp at the sheer speed of the train, the weight of it coming straight at me.

Close my eyes. Do it now.

The drop is fast, tinged with relief. It's safe down here. Already I'm deeper in than I like to be, but I hold onto the sense of where I am, edging my way through five minutes.

Safe, now. I slide forwards a little more, just to be sure, before I pull up to the surface.

Sucking in air, I land between the tracks and stumble forwards before catching myself. Bright light and hard sunshine. The rush feels heavy this time.

I find my shorts and top, breathing hard, clear in my head now about what I was doing. I needed to prove this to myself as much as to the others. Maybe one day that freight train will be a police car, or even a bullet. Maybe. At least I know I can jump under pressure when I need to.

The climb is easier this time. Echo begins to clap before I've even dropped to the ground on the other side of the fence. Slow claps, nodding with each one. Amon claps faster, not holding back.

'Thought you'd chicken out,' says Boc and jerks his head to one side. 'Kudos.'

I rub the tops of my arms. 'Thanks.'

Mason is standing to one side, one hand still gripping the fence. When he sees me looking he sets his mouth straight, not giving anything away.

'Next train's not for an hour,' says Boc. 'Anyone want to wait?'

'Nah, time for us to get back,' says Amon. 'Our folks will be home soon.'

To my relief, everyone seems to take that as a cue to leave as well.

We start back across the park, the sun still strong. It's only when he taps my shoulder that I realise Mason has fallen in beside me.

As I turn to him, his hand slips back into his pocket. 'Hey,' he says.

'Hey.' I wait.

'You did good today.'

'Thanks.'

He doesn't say more after that, but he sticks by my side the whole way back in a way that makes it feel as if we're in all this together.

I'm not hungry when I get home, won't need to sleep tonight, but I start prepping the delivery so that dinner's ready when Mum comes home from a walk.

She's even more tired than usual so we don't talk much, but when she asks how I am it's easy to say, 'fine'. I don't have to put on some act that I'm okay. This must be how it feels to think that all is lost, only to realise that you're still alive.

CHAPTER NINETEEN

MUM SLEEPS LATE the next day. She's only in the mood for tea and toast when I ask. Easy, at least.

A few minutes later I carry over a steaming mug. 'You all right?' She's sitting up in bed, catching up on news reports. I sit beside her and cross my legs on top of the covers.

'Of course.' She rests the compad on her lap. 'Just a bit tired. Busy week. And ...' A sigh. 'I need to go away next week, sweetheart, for a work conference.'

'Cool. Like a holiday, except you have to work?' The conferences she's had before were via distance link-up.

'I'm sorry, Scout. They won't let me put it off any longer –'

'Put it off?'

'... they've been asking me for a while, but I don't feel comfortable leaving you alone.'

She's making way more out of this than she needs to. 'I'll be fine. Don't worry. That sounds like fun.' She rubs the back of her neck and I can tell she's still not sure. 'Mum, I'm fourteen. I can look after myself.'

That makes her lips scrunch to one side, still too pale and thin. She's spent so much of her life focused on me, she has trouble letting go.

'It'll be good for me, yeah?' I say, trying to show that I'm relaxed about it so she'll relax too.

'I'll speak to Alistair, ask him to check in with you,' Mum says. 'If you have any trouble, anything at all, ask him for help okay?'

'Sure.' Already I'm planning how far I'll jump, a few days maybe. But of course I don't say that.

'Should I ask Mrs Richardson as well?'

'Nah. That's okay.' I can tell that she's been fretting about this for a while. 'You'll be able to call, won't you?'

'Some nights.' She's sitting really still, just her eyes move to me. 'What will you do while I'm gone?'

'Mum, I told you. I'll be fine.'

'I mean, how will you pass the time?'

'I …' I don't know if I should tell her about my plans to time skip. We haven't spoken about it since the day after I showed her.

'Listen Scout, I've been thinking a lot about your … disappearing.'

I keep quiet, waiting until I see where she's going.

'Do you still think it might help you escape the authorities?' Mum asks.

'Yes.' The eagerness rises – there's so much I could share with her – but I keep it contained. 'It takes practice, but I'm getting better. If I have to jump quickly I'll be able to do it. And I can control how long I stay away, too …'

I break off, watching her closely. She's quiet for a bit, her body still.

Impatience gets the better of me. 'I thought you were okay with it now?'

'No.' But the smile creases have deepened around her eyes. 'I'm still not happy, but I don't want you keeping it from me either. I don't want to push you away, Coutlyn.'

'Mum.' There's reproach in my tone, telling her not to be silly. I place a hand on her knee beneath the doona, and she covers my hand with hers. An idea comes to me.

'Maybe this will help.' I grab my compad and shuffle closer so she can watch. 'See? If you go in here, and then tap on … this.' The grid appears on the screen, showing our two dots side-by-side. I tag my own and create a tracking bot. 'I'll set up the same shortcut on your compad. So all you have to do is tap on this icon, and you'll be able to see where I am. Even if you don't get a chance to call, you'll be able to see me.'

Mum's been quiet through each of the steps.

'And if you can't find me on the grid, that means I've time skipped. But I always come back to the same place, okay? You might have to wait a day or so, but you'll be able to see me return. You'll know I'm okay.'

Mum lifts a finger towards the screen. 'Show me how to get in again?'

'Like this? And then …' Step-by-step I take her through it

all once more while she nods and points. 'I'll set it up on your compad so you can check whenever you like.'

When I get to the end, her eyes soften and lift to meet mine. 'Okay. Good.'

———————

'Agent X, reporting for duty.'

It's Mum's first night away and I've just come home. I step around the entrance wall in the communal kitchen to see Alistair pulling on an oven mitt.

Haven't caught up with him for ages. 'How are you, Alistair?'

'Still working.' A pause, before his eyebrows go up. 'Hungry?'

'Nah, thanks. I'll be right.'

'Come on.' A stiff arm lifts towards the other side of the bench and gestures at a second place setting complete with a full glass of water. 'I made shepherd's pie. Just for you.'

He opens the oven, guiding out a single-serve ramekin with golden potato mash peaked above it. The steaming dish rests on a plate while Alistair turns slowly back and pulls out a second, golden brown just like the first. It's almost as if he was watching me on the grid and timed the meal for when I came home.

He settles on the edge of a stool, half standing and half leaning. It doesn't look comfortable. 'Bon appetit.'

What to say? My face is scrunched in its own torn push-pull. 'But I …' It would be rude to eat his food, but now that I see the second pie, it feels rude to refuse.

My eyebrows go up. 'Wait here, yeah?'

The pies would be burning hot anyway. I dash back to our room and click the cold cupboard open. Five leftover lentil balls will do just fine. Yoghurt dip blobs into a fresh bowl. A carrot quickly becomes a pile of colourful sticks. Nothing too flash but at least I'll be adding to the meal.

Alistair drops his chin when I return with my plate, glad that I've accepted his offer without a fuss.

The lentil balls are cold but taste okay smothered in sauce. We talk about the weather as we dip and chew, but I can't help wondering what he knows. If Alistair was watching the grid to check when I'd be home, what else has he seen on my history map? And how much has Mum told him already?

The pie makes my brain melt, it's so good. Pretty sure it's lab steak but you wouldn't know, apart from the way the chunks fall apart in uniform segments. Not that I've had real steak for a while. I think the last time it was affordable enough for Mum was my seventh birthday. We're halfway through when we run out of small talk.

I jump in before he does. 'So how's work?' I ask breezily.

Alistair swallows, clears his throat. 'Fine, still keeping me busy.'

'Found the cure for cancer yet?' Worth a try.

No reaction other than crinkles deepening at the corners of his eyes.

'Solved the famine crisis?' I try again.

'Something like that.' One side of his mouth kinks up, enjoying the mystery that remains around his job no matter how many ways I ask.

There's still about a quarter of his pie left when Alistair leans back, pushing his plate towards the centre of the bench. He takes a sip of water.

'How's your mother?' he asks.

Not what I was expecting, but at least we're getting somewhere. He would have spoken to her himself. 'She's okay. Busy, I think.'

'She worries, you know.'

And here we are. I decide to come right out and ask. 'How much has she told you?'

'Your mother told me … something quite extraordinary.' His eyes travel from his plate to rest on me. 'I spent a lot of time checking the grid to make sense of what I was seeing.'

'And?' Already, I'm standing. 'Want to see for yourself?'

'No.' His face darkens. 'No, Scout. Sit.'

Back on the stool, disappointed but still eager to talk about it with him, I lean forwards. 'But you saw on the grid, right? You can see it's real. What do you think about that?'

Alistair considers me for a moment.

'I think …' he starts, then breaks off. 'The truth is I don't know what to think.' He shuffles on the stool. 'Whatever this thing is that you've found, it needs to be studied, understood –'

'Yeah, I know …' I'm leaning forwards, eager to join in but again he cuts me off.

'… in controlled conditions, with safety systems. This thing is dangerous in the hands of kids. You have no idea what you're dealing with.'

My shoulders lift, because he's right in some ways, but I end up shaking my head. 'That's just because you haven't done it yourself.' Nothing that feels that good could be dangerous.

Now it's Alistair's turn to lean forwards. Slowly. Creaking. 'But you don't know, Scout –'

Yes, I do. I think about being lost in the tunnel that day. But I made it out, didn't I? It's our own mind, our fears, that hold us back.

'You're only a few weeks away from beginning at your new school. You don't want to jeopardise that opportunity.'

'No.' Head shaking. 'No. It's okay, Alistair. I promise you. It will be okay.'

We're quiet for a bit. Alistair takes a sip of water so I lift my glass too. I'm thirstier than I realised.

'How are you feeling about school?' he asks after a while.

'Can't wait.' I place the glass on the bench and find myself smiling at him. 'I couldn't have managed it without you. Any of it, really.' In my mind I move through all the ways he's helped me. Getting into school. Understanding the grid. How to make the chip my own.

'I worry, sometimes,' Alistair sighs. 'Perhaps I've sent you down a path of no return.'

'Wouldn't have it any other way.' And now that I'm saying it, I realise how true that is. Other than Mason, I don't think I'd change a thing even if I could. If I'd been a citizen, I'd never have stolen the chip, and never would have learnt how to time skip.

That last thought is enough to make up my mind. I push back

the stool and stand. 'Stay there.' I step around to the opposite side of the bench from Alistair. 'I'm going to show you for real. Just this once.'

Creases deepen on his forehead, but he stays quiet. Curious, perhaps.

Two steps back, I kneel so that I can see his head and nothing more above the bench, which means that he can see the same of me.

A quick glance along the hall: no sign of the Richardsons. Then back to look at Alistair with a smile of reassurance, before I drop away.

Only a few seconds later I'm back, breathing hard and smiling at the rush of it. I slip on my clothes in seconds.

Alistair hasn't moved, other than his lips parting.

Can't help the corners of my mouth lifting and as they do, Alistair matches my expression. Amazed.

'I could teach you, if you'd like,' I try. 'You'd be able to see further into the future than you ever would otherwise.'

He blinks three or four times quickly and I wish I could take back the words I just said. What was I thinking? Talking about his mortality like that.

Then he shakes his head. 'I think I've already glimpsed it, Agent X. Just then, you showed the future to me.'

Mum comes home really flat at the end of her conference, her skin this pale shade of grey and her hair limp as if it hasn't even been washed. She doesn't want to talk about the conference much so I don't push, but when I show her the credits I saved by time skipping, she relaxes and even smiles. We'll pay back our debt sooner than we thought. I'm nearly 500 credits ahead of where I'd be if I'd stayed and, you know, done stuff and eaten food.

She only seems to have checked the grid a few times, so when she asks about my time skipping I'm glad to fill her in. I managed to skip nearly forty hours after my evening with Alistair. Soon after returning from that, I skipped ahead three whole days. Feeling my way forwards is easier now. Each long jump seems to open up the possibility of jumping further again.

Mum listens while I talk about my time skipping, elbows on knees and her mouth in a straight line. She's not relaxed about it, exactly, but accepting at least.

She even gives the green light for me to keep practising, as long as I warn her when I'll be away and promise an evening or lunch date together each time I come back. So I find myself free to keep skipping further as the summer continues, playing with the sense of possibility opening out before me while my days disappear like playing cards in the wind.

After my longest jump, over a week, I find that I need to settle before leaving again. So I head over to the rock-climbing centre to compare notes with the others, and even do a few smaller skips with them while I'm there. The others have managed a couple of long skips, too, using summer camp or visits to friends' houses as excuses. Amon and Boc have been working on a technique where they skip from halfway up the climbing wall, returning with sharp enough response to catch the handholds and stop themselves from falling. Mason's super accurate with his returns, almost able to make it to the exact second. Echo is pretty much an all-rounder; as soon as someone does something new she's the first to match. And me? I'm not the best at anything, but at least I'm able to keep up. That's all I need to do.

Before we even know it, we're a week away from the first day of school. No wonder the time passed so quickly, we've skipped so many days.

'You're ready,' Boc says when Amon returns from a clear five minutes after Mason shot the gun at the rock-climbing centre.

'Yeah.' Amon keeps moving, breathing hard as he pulls on a shirt. 'Yeah. I know.'

'Well?'

'He should wait until he wants to go,' Mason calls from the other side of the room.

'Nah, it's okay.' Amon glances towards Echo, halfway up the climbing wall. 'I'm ready. Let's do this.'

Mason jumped on the freight tracks soon after I did, and Echo in a moment of exasperation, I think, as a way to dampen Boc's ego after he was first to skip longer than a week. So Amon's jump today isn't just training, it's also the final challenge left to us before the holidays end.

We head out as a group, tracing the familiar path to the freight tracks.

'That last jump was a bit of a shock, don't you think?' Echo says once we're all through the gap in the fence. 'We left in the middle of the heat wave, and then when we came back there was all that smoke, people walking around with masks over their mouths. Freaked me out. Didn't know what was going on until we got home.'

'Yeah, what did Dad call it?' Amon calls from a few steps ahead.

'Time lag,' Echo says from beside me. 'Like jet lag, but with no news reports when you get there.'

'Hang on,' I say. 'Your parents know?'

'Yep.' Echo pauses as the path narrows between two eucalypts, letting me through first. 'They've even managed a couple of short skips.'

'Didn't they lose the plot when you told them?' I say over my shoulder, thinking of Mum.

Echo jogs to catch up. 'Yeah, at first. But they're way obsessed with studying it now. Practising any chance they can get.'

From a few steps ahead, Mason and Amon are still talking about longer jumps.

'When you think about it, each new day has always been hidden til you get there,' Mason is saying. 'For everyone, I mean. Even without time skipping, you still have no idea what's waiting tomorrow. You just get there faster.'

'Yeah, except you know how things are today at least,' from Amon. 'So you get … like, clues about what's about to change. It's more gradual. So it's not such a shock.'

'The further we jump, the less we'll know what's waiting

when we land,' says Mason. 'And the longer we're away the harder it will be to adjust once we arrive.' He glances back to me and I know what he's thinking. The woman who died had jumped seventeen years. What must that have been like?

'That means with leaps of more than a few days there's no way to know what's coming, no real way to prepare?' says Amon.

'So what?' Boc's been quiet, until now. 'Most people don't prepare for anything anyway. The dinosaurs who still live day by day, most of them don't realise that anything's changing. Not until it's too late.'

'Dinosaurs?' I can't help asking. 'Like, your parents and most of your friends, you mean?'

'I've asked them if they want to learn but most of them think I'm crazy. The only ones who seem to get it are Amon's folks. So, like I said ...' Boc drifts off.

We're quiet for a bit, walking through the scrub of the open parkland. The conversation drops away as Boc and Amon organise some sort of catch-up tomorrow, an early-morning climb I think. The only sound is the squawking of a flock of cockatoos in the distance.

'How about five in the morning?' asks Boc. 'Before it's too hot?'

Silence from Amon before he asks, 'How about six?'

'Five thirty?' says Boc. 'We'll see the sunrise and everything.'

A snort from Amon as we reach the fence line overlooking the freight tracks. 'All right, you win. Who needs sleep? Five thirty it is.'

It's still dry, but not as hot as it has been. Amon drops his backpack and starts circling his shoulders and neck as preparation. We all have our quirky ways to prepare, clearing a throat or clicking knuckles, finding a way to focus.

'See ya in a bit.' Amon flicks Echo's ponytail so that it hits her in the face.

She musses up his hair. 'Likewise, boofhead.'

We send him off with claps and calls of good luck then watch as Amon makes his way down to the tracks. It's not long until the 3.17 train, so the conversation drops away as he finds his place on the tracks. It will all happen so quickly when the train finally arrives. We all understand how intense it is to have the massive bullet shooting straight for you.

We've been watching for a while when Mason checks his compad. 'Must be running late,' he says. 'It's nineteen past.'

Amon must have checked the time as well because after another few minutes he starts back up the slope towards us. Mason's been busy on his compad, checking the situation.

'It's still coming,' Mason calls once Amon is part way up the slope. 'Just running late. About ten minutes from what I can tell.'

Amon nods and heads back to his place on the tracks. It must feel a bit like an anticlimax, after psyching himself up for a skip.

The next few minutes pass in silence, agonisingly slowly.

'How long now?' mumbles Boc.

'It's hard to tell,' Mason says, still busy with his compad, just as I hear the high hum.

In the next instant it's here, a series of silver and white.

We're all at the fence. 'Did anyone see?' I ask.

'He jumped,' says Echo. 'I saw him jump.'

Flashes of light and dark pass by, so many carriages moving so incredibly fast. It must be at least three or four minutes before the last carriage disappears from sight as suddenly as it appeared.

We watch in silence, relief waiting just a few moments from where we are now. Now that the train's gone, we can see the neat pile of Amon's clothes in the middle of the track. He made the jump, now all he has to do is return.

Time slips steadily past.

Boc's the first to shift away from the fence, finding a place on the picnic table. Each minute seems to slide slower than the last. I'm itching to check the time but I don't, not wanting to bring focus to this sense of him being away too long.

It must be about twenty minutes before any of us speaks. 'When's the next train?' Boc asks finally.

Now that he's broken the quiet, we all start at once.

'… never stayed away this long unless he meant it.'

'I saw him jump. He's just slow to return –'

Mason lifts his head from his compad. 'Next train is a few minutes past four.'

'So, he just has to come back before then,' Echo says, her voice faint. 'No big deal.'

A minute later she starts climbing the fence. 'I'm going down.' If Amon comes back in a daze she'll be able to help him off the tracks.

'I'll come,' Boc says.

I sit at the picnic table, watching Boc and Echo make their way towards the tracks. Too many of us down there might attract attention.

'Can you reconnect the safety sensors?' I ask Mason.

'Already done it.' He's leaning against the fence, hands in pockets. He turns from the tracks to me. 'Think this is what happened to you?'

'Don't know. Maybe.' By now Boc and Echo have crouched behind a control box near the tracks. 'It's like … you get lost or something. I don't know.'

'But you found your way back.'

'Yeah.' I check the tracks again and breathe in. 'So, worst thing that can happen is that he returns and triggers the safety sensor.' But I can tell from the way Mason keeps tapping the tips of his fingers together that he's thought of worse things that could happen.

We watch in numb silence as the train arrives and continues past. Echo goes to stand while Boc holds her shoulders, sort of in a hug but also holding her back. If Amon returns while the train's passing, even the safety sensors won't be enough to save him.

Then it's gone, and we're left with the same empty space as before.

Echo refuses to leave even when it gets dark, so Mason and I head back to his place for sleeping bags, food and water.

Mum's so used to me time skipping by now that she asks no questions when I message her that I'll be home the next day.

When we get back with the gear, we eat little and talk less, taking turns behind the control box to watch the spot where Amon last stood.

The last train passes at about one in the morning. On the timetable there's a break of about five hours, I guess as loading bays shut down for the night. We could skip ahead until the first train, or go home of course. But none of us do.

He's about to come back any second, isn't he? Until that happens we're stuck together in this strange limbo.

It's one of those still summer nights with wisps of cloud lit up by the moon. I doze a little, using my arm as a pillow on top of the picnic table. I don't think the others sleep at all. Boc sticks beside Echo the whole time, resting a hand on her shoulder when he sees her staring into the distance, saying the same thing, over and over. 'It will be okay.'

Watching him with her through these long hours almost makes me forgive him for everything. Only almost, though. Because I can't help thinking that he's the one who set up this training exercise and talked Amon into it. It's Boc who got us into this.

When first light breaks, we're at the fence again. Mason's down at the control box, his legs stretched lazily at his front. There's still another half hour before the first train. My gaze is drawn to the spot in case Amon somehow returned while we weren't watching.

All I find is his pile of clothes.

The lid of the night lifts off the world and details sharpen around us. I crack a can of water to drink and offer it to the others. Maybe the new dawn will be enough to call Amon back.

It's only when Echo gasps beside me that I turn to see some sort of maintenance trolley clacking slowly along the tracks. A lone figure stands on it, near the front, his torso lit with flickering blue from a control panel in front of him.

Mason's body stiffens as he sees, and he sucks himself into a ball, hidden behind the control box.

Already I'm on the grid, searching for access to the trolley coms, a way to override perhaps, but all I find is the dot on the grid for the maintenance worker. The control panel for the trolley is hidden behind a firewall.

With slow clacks, the trolley continues. It reaches Amon's pile of clothes, slows, then stops with a clunk. You can almost hear the maintenance worker wondering what he's found. For agonising seconds he cranes his neck, looking down at the pile of clothes. I can sense his confusion from here.

Mason shifts behind the control box. Not sure what he should do. Why didn't we hide the clothes?

The maintenance worker swipes at the control pad. The trolley clicks, and begins to move forwards. My eyes close with relief.

An inhale from Echo, and I open my eyes as she gasps, 'No.'

The trolley has again stopped, right above the pile of clothes.

A red light flares underneath, starting at one side and moving towards the other. Scanning.

We all start moving, but with no clear sense of purpose. Down near the tracks, Mason stands. I grab for my compad; maybe I can find a workaround to get that trolley moving. A change in the atmosphere makes me turn to see sunlight slip over the rooftops to the east.

It's only when Mason calls out that I turn back again. At first I don't understand the shape that has appeared at the base of the trolley.

It can't be …

'Jump NOW. Amon! You have to JUMP AGAIN!' Mason's voice is shrill, cracked with desperation, lunging towards the trolley. He stumbles before finding his footing again.

The maintenance worker cries out in alarm, jumping off the trolley at Mason's appearance, but I barely notice him.

All I can do is watch, my mind sliding and falling, as Amon returns, his head and torso emerging from the tray of the trolley in a way that doesn't make sense. My mouth falls open, brain can't understand. Amon's head drops back as his body slumps.

Still Mason screams, 'JUMP! NOW!' He reaches the trolley and pulls to a stop. Almost as soon as he makes it there, he begins to retreat, his each step pushed back by a creeping pool of red.

CHAPTER TWENTY

I'M HALFWAY UP the fence before I know what I'm doing, the wire rocking and clanging as the others climb beside me. A whimper from Echo as she lands is our only sound, because what words are there?

Already she's scrambling down the slope ahead of me. Sprinting now. Somehow, I manage to stay close, faster than Boc. All I can think is that I have to be there when she reaches Amon, to save her somehow from what she's about to find.

We race past Mason staring dumbly at the trolley, his arms hanging limp at his sides. The maintenance worker is on the other side of the tracks, about twenty metres away by now, swiping frantically at a compad, no doubt calling for backup.

We reach the circle of red but Echo doesn't hesitate, our steps crunching wet over soil soaked with blood. A leap onto the trolley and to a sudden stop; momentum threatens to carry me forwards, but my knees absorb the shock. My heart is choking.

I'm still trying to make sense of the figure slumped at our feet when Echo gasps and spins away, palms over her eyes. Already I'm with her, holding her tight, a hand at the back of her neck, feeling her jerk with each sob. We're pushed so close that I'm rocked by each shudder, accepting the emotion into my body. I'd take it all if I could.

Slowly, my eyes track to the figure at our feet. Amon's torso is slumped forwards, arms pinned at an angle that is so wrong, his skin pale in the morning light. It shouldn't be that colour, a strange ashen grey. Where are Amon's legs? Meshed around the base of the trolley? Only when I close my eyes do I realise that they're brimmed with tears.

My eyes open to find the day growing around us, the sunlight strengthening. Hasn't the world stopped?

Echo is quiet now, empty. I guide her down from the trolley. Don't glance down, don't think about what we're stepping on.

'Stay where you are,' the maintenance worker calls, his voice shrill and uncertain. He's on the phone on his compad, receiving instructions.

Boc is waiting with Mason; he reaches out for Echo and encloses her in a hug before turning to me, hand lifting with palm up. *What do we do?*

But I can't look at him now, can't respond. Instead I blink at the compad and try to find some sort of focus, a way to cut through this chaos. Already the maintenance worker has triggered an emergency alert, tagging all of us. *Dangerous suspects.* Ambulance. Police. Everyone's coming.

What are we going to do?

Mason's face says it all, dust streaked with wet lines, his forehead tight with pain. 'I told him to jump. He didn't even realise … I'm not sure –'

'It's okay,' I say, even though nothing is okay. 'An ambulance is coming,' I add, falling quiet with the emptiness of the words. Can't help checking Echo. She's looking at me but I don't think she's focusing.

The worker is holding an arm out straight, a warning for us to stay back, clutching his compad in the other hand.

Still, Echo is watching me, vague and confused. 'What's that sound?'

From all around us comes a pulsing rumble. 'Drones,' Boc calls, just as Mason points to three cars approaching from behind the maintenance worker.

'Oh crap, it's the Feds,' breathes Boc.

They're parked before I can even step back, people in black padded uniforms emerging, already coming at us. How did they get here so fast?

'Hands behind your heads! Stay where you are!'

Five or six of the officers advance towards us with pistols aimed, visors masking their faces. One of them holds a compad, checking the grid and shouting orders at the others. Their sheer speed and efficiency send my heart racing.

'Hands behind your heads!' shouts the officer with the compad. He points to Mason. 'You! On the ground! Face down!'

Mason steps back, too stunned to respond, his face tight with fear. I've never seen anyone so scared.

Still the Feds move towards us. 'Mason,' I whisper. Because, what are we going to do?

He blinks, before turning to me. 'Midnight,' he breathes. Then, 'Midnight?'

A glance at the officers is the only response I can manage, too scared to speak. I turn to make sure the others heard as Mason drops to his knees, and then lies on his stomach. One of the officers rushes forwards and cuffs his wrists behind him; he's so helpless now that all he can do is turn his head to me. He raises his eyebrows.

So I nod, slowly at first then faster and faster. *Yes, I understand.* His head turns away.

Then he's gone. Just his clothes remain as if laid out ready for a new day, the cuffs resting neatly on the shorts.

All is still around us.

Two of the officers step back and turn to each other. The one with the compad pulls up his visor, his eyes tracing over the space where Mason used to be.

We could run, I think in a flash. But I'm not thinking straight; I'm thinking like someone who can't skip.

'Don't MOVE! Stay where you ARE!' the officer barks at us, his words even sharper, even more urgent than before.

Somehow it brings the other officers back, their pistols aim fresh, the attention on us all but centred on Boc. The stakes are higher now, and my heart races faster.

One glance sideways, and I know. Boc's gone in a blink, his clothes falling where he stood.

Shock doesn't win us any time the way it did with Mason. The circle shrinks around us, the steps ever closer.

'Stay where you are! I said, no moving! Stay WHERE YOU ARE!' The main officer's fear makes him somehow more terrifying.

Echo makes a squeak, her eyes wide, and drops away.

Still they come at me, still yelling. My hands are shaking. I push out a breath and find the place where all is calm.

Just let go.

It's dark, but there's a half moon, so it's not completely black. The air is still and cool around me. Sharp twigs and dirt at my feet. No clothes, but even worse, my compad is gone. The rush is quickly chased by a hard return to reality.

Mason's here already, his skin pale in the moonlight as he brushes loose soil from his knees and palms. Boc and Echo return within seconds of each other, their chests lifting and falling in time.

Echo's gaze lifts towards the rail tracks and we all turn in silence. Police tape encloses the area but nothing remains. The air feels heavy with absence.

'You okay?' I ask Mason.

'Yeah.' He closes his eyes, still adjusting. Remembering, maybe.

'Let's go,' mutters Boc. 'We don't have much time.'

In silence we make our way up the slope, numbly following

behind. For some reason our overnight bags are still where we stashed them, under the picnic table, so we share out a mishmash of clothes, tops for the girls, bottoms for the boys, and begin our way across the park.

Only four of us are returning the way we came; there should be five.

'Want me to take you home?' I ask Echo gently.

'No. Not yet.' Her voice is tight, her movements contained.

It gives me the sense that she wants to be alone, so I pull back and fall in beside Mason. He jerks his chin my way, a sad sort of welcome. So I stick by his side, matching my strides with his. Without really thinking what I'm doing I rest a hand on his shoulder, offering comfort, or perhaps asking for some.

He glances my way briefly as his other hand lifts to rest on mine, trapping my fingers the way he did when we first time skipped together.

We stay that way only a few strides before Mason lifts my hand from his shoulder, guiding it down so that his other hand can close around it. His grip is firm, warm. Maybe, in some other world, I might have wondered what it could mean, begun hoping about a future together. But life now exists for us only in terms of minutes ahead. How long until we hear that pulsing throb return. How long until we're discovered again.

After a while our grip shifts at the same time, loosening only enough for our fingers to interlace, hands locked even firmer.

No idea what the future holds, but for now we're never letting go.

Boc finds a way in to the rock-climbing centre from a side entrance. Pretty sure he's done this before. The comscreen at reception flickers to life and Mason settles in, a sense of urgency growing now that we have access to the grid.

Echo finds a space on the floor and slumps with her back against a wall, not focusing on much. It makes me wonder which nightmare keeps playing in her mind, the one she just lived through or the one she'll have to face when she sees her parents. I'm beginning to realise why she's in no hurry to go home.

I find a spare chair in a back room and wheel it out to Mason. Boc stands to see over his other shoulder.

Already Mason has the grid on the screen. We all lean forwards at the same time. Little orange circles rim each of our dots. *Wanted for questioning* comes up when Mason hovers the cursor over my dot. Same for Echo and Boc.

When it hovers over Mason's dot though, all air leaves my chest. *Arrest warrant.*

I'm out of the chair and across the room, biting my lip as I check out the entrance doors. No approaching lights that I can find. No rumble of engines coming this way. But how long do we have?

And then what?

It's only now that it's happening for real that I realise that time skipping will only get us so far. Each time we return we'll be tagged and pursued again. But for how long? They'll eventually work out that we have to return to the same spot. We can't keep jumping forever.

'Finished?' I ask, coming back to the reception desk. 'We have to go.'

'Hold on.' By now Mason has a new screen on view, trying to hack in to the server at the Federal Police.

Soon he leans back. 'Dammit. Can't get in.'

'Here.' I pull the keyboard close and get busy.

'Scout, I need the comscreen.' Mason's hand is firm on my arm, just this side of annoyance.

'One minute.' Back to the grid, I set up a fresh alert to tell us if anyone's approaching from about three kms out. We're in an industrial estate so no-one else should be here at this time of night.

When I've finished, I push the keyboard back towards Mason. 'There. It's all yours. But if you hear an alarm it means the police are coming.'

His mouth is pushed to one side, not annoyed anymore. 'Actually … that gives me an idea.'

I stay quiet as I watch, no distractions slowing him down. Instead of trying to find a way into the main server, Mason goes back to the grid, his thin hands moving quickly as he traces a path in reverse, finding the server that added the arrest warrant, then patching his way back in via the instruction path. Clever. It's like sneaking into a building through an exit door by having someone open it from the inside.

Soon we're trawling through the files on the server at the

Federal Police, reading through notes that mention our names. There's not much on Boc, Echo and me, most of it seems to reference back to Mason, but the files on him are a whole new story. I don't understand half of the phrases used – *felony*, *reckless endangerment* – but I understand others, like *suspect* and *wilful damage*. *Manslaughter*.

After a while Mason's hands drop to his lap, his head lowered. Boc has his arms crossed, jaw muscles clenched as he stares at the screen. Soon his chest expands and slowly contracts.

'So ... what?' I ask. 'They're trying to blame Mason for ...?' I glance at Echo. I don't have to say it.

'Sort of. Not –' Boc glances at Echo too, 'not premeditated or anything. But –'

'But they know I'm the one who blocked the safety sensors.' Mason lifts his head. 'So they're going to hang a case off that.'

'But ...' Head shaking. 'It wasn't your idea. It was –' My sightline lifts to Boc and I break off as I realise this is the first time I've looked him in the eye since the accident. The guy who knows no fear. He's the reason why Mason cut the safety sensors; he's the reason why Amon was taking such a risk. If the police are looking for someone to blame, it should be Boc.

Boc sees me watching and crosses his arms, pushing his chin forwards. *Got something to say?*

Can't sit anymore. I'm up and at the entrance doors, looking into the night. The alarm is set to warn us if anyone's coming, but I have to see for myself. Black night is close around us. I lean my shoulder against the glass.

Mason and Boc keep talking in low voices. 'This is bad. I think they have a case.'

'We won't let them get you, Mase.'

My eyes drop and I trace a finger over the raised lump of the chip scar. It's been faded by the procedure, but it's still new in so many ways.

'We've been talking about it already, haven't we?' whispers Boc. 'Now we have a reason.'

No reply at first, then Mason asks, 'You think we would make it?'

'Only one way to find out.'

My hands drop as I stand away from the door. I knew it would be useful to go off-grid. Just didn't realise how much.

'You have to cut it out,' I call across the room. 'Your chip, I mean. Or write some sort of masking code.'

Mason looks up from the comscreen. 'What?'

'Your chip. It's the reason they can track you, right? So we cut it out, leave it here. Or find a way to block it from the grid. When they come, you'll be long gone.' As I talk, I make my way to the reception desk and stop in front of it. 'You'll be free.'

'Free?' His forehead creases. 'With no water? No access to food?'

'I know a water source. We'll work food out. The important thing is you'll be safe once you're off-grid.'

'Off-grid,' Mason mumbles, the creases deepening around his eyes. Except he's not talking to me, he just said that to thin air.

I shuffle sideways, trying to catch his sightline. 'I've been working on a masking code, but it re-triggers whenever you move. Maybe if we had more time, but we don't. I think cutting the chip out is the only way.'

'I'm not …' Mason snaps out of his thoughts and sighs. 'Scout, I'm not cutting out my chip. I …' He turns to Boc. 'We have a plan.'

Echo's still leaning against the wall but I can tell that she's listening. I turn back to find Mason waiting for me.

Slowly, he inhales. 'We're going to time skip further than ever before,' Mason says, emphasising each word. 'So far that none of this will be on file anymore. The case will be long closed.'

'How far?' Echo asks from behind me on the floor.

'Ten years.' From Boc. 'More if we need.'

But I'm not looking at the others, all that I see right now is Mason. 'You've talked about this?'

'Sort of. Yes. But it's different now.' He makes his way around the reception desk to me. 'It's sooner than we thought, but … don't you see? This is where we've been heading all along.'

My eyes lower, scanning the worn tiles. He'd be safe, I guess. Boc would go with him. But what sort of world would they find? Water supplies could have diminished even more than they are now. Rations might be even tighter.

Then again, maybe not. They'd have their parents waiting for them. And me, I guess. For all I know, life might be better in ten years …

I risk a peek sideways. 'You think you could make it that far?' I ask.

A cautious smile. 'We know it's possible, yeah? We've seen that woman make seventeen years. Who knows? Maybe we could go ten times as far.'

His gaze is so even, his face so open that I know without having to ask. He *wants* to do this. He's not just jumping as an escape, but also to see what he'll find.

It's too much, too fast. Even though it would keep him safe from the police, I can't help a lump rising in my throat. 'But as far as we know there's no coming back –'

'I know.' He says it softly.

He'd still be sixteen, and I'd be twenty-four.

'Come with us.' Mason's close by now, his hand at the tip of my elbow. When I lift my head, his mouth opens again but before the words have formed an alarm rings out from the comscreen. We all go still.

In the next instant, we're moving at once. Mason and I bolt around the reception desk while Echo jumps up from the floor.

Hands shaking, I bring up the grid map of the industrial estate and zoom out. Twenty or so dots from all around us are headed this way.

CHAPTER TWENTY-ONE

'THIS WAY,' CALLS BOC.

Echo is beside him already, heading for one of the side doors. I'm halfway across the room when I realise Mason's not with me. I spin back to find him typing and mouthing to himself as he peers at the comscreen.

Through the entrance doors I catch a flash of distant headlights. The windows are rattling with vibrations from the approaching drones.

'Mason,' I hiss.

'Hold on.'

The others have stopped too. Boc strides towards the reception desk. 'Mase, we gotta go.'

'Nearly … finished …' Mason mumbles, furiously typing between each word.

'Mason.' I'm close by now, a hand on my forehead as I examine the screen. 'Hang on.' I realise that the lines on the screen are familiar. It's the masking code that I was playing with as a way of dropping off-grid. 'Where did you get that from?'

Mason's eyes don't leave the screen. 'You said you'd been working on it at home.'

He's hacked into my home comscreen and copied the script. Except he's made some changes too. Just a simple few lines of code that are so elegant I can't help being impressed. Soon Mason copies the same code from his dot on the grid to mine, and then Boc's.

By now the others are watching over Mason's shoulder. Finally the code is added to Echo's dot. Mason clicks to bring up the grid map in real time. 'Look.'

Gridlines spread across the screen showing reception at the rock-climbing centre, exactly where we are now. Except …

From either side I feel Echo and Boc lean closer. None of our dots are visible. Not one for any of us.

Already Mason is grinning. 'You're a genius, Scout. That code you wrote to hide from being seen on the grid? I made some changes so that we stay masked as we move around.'

I step backwards then forwards, testing, then check the screen. Nothing.

'So it looks like we're not here?' asks Echo.

'Better.' Mason tilts his head. 'It will look like we jumped, right? So they'll be watching for our return while we're still getting away.' He turns to Boc. 'We'll be able to organise supplies. See our folks.'

Boc nods and rolls his shoulders as if preparing for work. 'Sort our stuff out. This is great.'

I can't believe he fixed the problem so easily. 'So, you'll be safe? You won't have to jump?'

Mason's mouth goes straight. 'No, the dots will only stay masked until we swipe for something. The minute you access water, food … swipe for anything and you'll be back on the grid. That's the best I can do.'

It was perhaps too much to ask. Here we are once more, the story of my life. There's freedom in being off-grid, but no life without rations.

Boc reaches over to take screen control, zooming out to see the area around this building. 'So why are they still coming?'

Only a kilometre away, twenty or so dots are making their way towards us. Still coming. The floor vibrates with their engines.

'Dammit,' snaps Mason. 'Why aren't they watching the grid? They should have seen us drop off.'

'Maybe they *are* watching the grid,' Echo says slowly. 'And they think that we've jumped. But they're still coming so they can secure the building for when we return.'

It takes only a second's thought before we react. She's right.

I waste precious seconds wiping Mason's coding history, before shutting down the comscreen. Then we're out the side door and into the climbing room, close behind Boc. Can't still be in the building when they lock it down. Even if we're hidden, we can't risk being trapped.

By now the engines are so close I can feel them in my stomach, a low, rumbling growl. We're heading for a side entrance when light flashes in through the glass panel, our legs caught in the beam before we duck to one side.

We're in a row, backs against the wall. From the front, Boc wiggles a pointer finger from side to side, meaning 'no'. Then he points back the way he came, taking the lead as we make our way to the rear.

When we make it to the back, light is rimming that door too. We're trapped.

Boc lifts his finger to his lips, then points back the way we came before stretching his arm above his head. His idea is to climb one of the walls, I guess, and make our way to the roof.

My heart is pounding so much that I think I might throw up, but I'm not sure if it's because of the police closing in on the building, or the idea of climbing one of those stupid walls.

Boc leads us to the room where we've been training all summer, and points up to a manhole in the ceiling next to the top of the climbing wall. It's dark in here, no lights on of course, just one long, high window allowing moonlight in.

Already Echo is halfway up the wall, her limbs somehow longer than I thought they were with each stretch for a new hold. Without a word Mason begins after her, not quite as smoothly but with the confidence of someone who's done this before.

I turn to Boc, and point. *You go.* Maybe I can follow behind and copy what he does.

He barely reacts, before he begins up the wall.

One foot on the place where Boc's just was, reaching out a hand to match his. But already I'm not sure where to reach, my grip weakening from angst about what I have to achieve. I'm barely off the floor.

It's only when I find Boc next to me that I realise he's climbed back down. 'What the hell are you doing?' he hisses. 'You're putting us all in danger.'

'I don't know how to climb,' I whisper.

'Then do exactly what I say,' he snaps.

'But …' Should I admit this? 'I'm a bit … not so good with heights.'

Boc's eyes narrow as he leans towards me in the dim light. 'Do what I say, when I say it, and we'll both get out of here.'

Okay. There's not much else I can do. One foot up, I reach a hand out to grasp one of the blobs sticking out from the wall. Step up to the next lump in the wall. It helps that I'm in bare feet, better able to feel my grip.

From one side, Boc whispers instructions each time I pause. 'Move your left hand up to that hold. Step sideways. Try swapping your hold the other way.'

Before I know it, I'm halfway up the wall. *Don't look down.* Just hold onto his voice.

When we're nearing the top, the smash of breaking glass echoes from reception. They're here, and they're coming in.

Before I can stop myself I glance down to the side door, making sure they're not opening it, too. Even though it's dark, the hugeness of the space below rushes up to me. The world lurches sideways and gravity sucks me away from the wall.

A whimper escapes my throat. Eyes closed, cheek pressed against the brick.

'Scout.' Through the panic I hear Boc: 'You're nearly there.'

'I …' Can't think. Can't breathe. 'I can't.'

'You can. And you will.'

Still, I don't move. Have to keep going, but no idea how to get my limbs moving again.

'Scout, the Feds are in the other room, okay? They're too busy securing reception to realise we're here.'

I don't understand how those words are the right ones, but somehow I find the courage to let go and reach immediately for the hold above.

One foot up, and then the other. I'm nearly at the rim when I pull up to find a hand reaching for me. Mason.

My fingers slip into his and I push off to feel the welcome lift as I make it over the edge. Panting, but here, with a solid platform beneath me. Made it, at last.

Boc pulls himself over the rim and slips open the manhole in the ceiling above us, motioning for us to follow. In silence we shuffle through the ceiling cavity. Boc replaces the manhole cover and dusty steps take us up through another door to the roof.

Clear sky is above us; headlights and voices beneath. Boc points, and we follow in silence. Warehouse roofs stretch so far ahead of us that I can't pick the end. They've been built in a row, with no gaps between, but it's nearly half an hour before we make it to the warehouse at the opposite end.

Boc takes us down through a door from the roof like the one on top of the climbing centre. We emerge into a storage facility stocked full with shelves of boxes up to the ceiling, which is about as high as the climbing wall was. The ladder down is short, only five or six rungs until we reach the next storey and have to track sideways for the next ladder along. It's not so bad as long as I don't think about what I'm doing.

Soon we're on the ground, eight or nine warehouses between us and the action at the other end. Out of sight, and off-grid.

Together we make our way to the edge of the industrial estate, streetlights and the glow of the sky showing the way.

At a fork in the track, we pause. One path will lead the others to the old highway and down to Moonee Ponds; the other way will take me to the Maribyrnong Canal, and home.

It must be three or four in the morning, quiet and dark. From here, you can see the whole city silhouetted against the moonlit sky, somehow different now, although I know it's not the city that has changed. It makes me wonder how much of the scene before us will still be here ten years from now. How much will be new? Just the idea of it makes my mind slow, my heart go steady and calm, the same as when you look into the sky and feel so small but part of something at the same time.

'So. When? Where?' asks Boc, rubbing his hands together.

'Think we should get a decent night's sleep,' Mason says. 'Who knows what kind of world we'll land in.'

'Midnight, two nights from now?'

Finding a time for them to leave is easy, but sorting out a place proves more difficult. Buildings might be pulled down; parks might be built over. After seeing what we've seen, the location of their return becomes the most important detail. Even the barest patch of dirt in a corner of nowhere might end up with a shrub growing in it.

They've been dancing over all the places that wouldn't work, when I lift my head. 'There's a cave near the entrance to Footscray Park. I used to use it as a water source.'

'Yeah?'

All three of them wait. 'It's too dark for anything to grow, and they wouldn't build because of the underground spring.'

Boc steps forwards. 'Whereabouts?'

'It's ...' Then I remember. 'It's where I found that woman. The one who ...' I trail off.

Mason pushes his mouth to one side. 'You mean there's an underground spring where you found her?'

'Yeah. I used to drink from there all the time.'

Creases deepening around his eyes as he stares at me. 'Do you think she knew?' Mason asks, as if I've been withholding information.

My hands lift helplessly in reply.

'It just seems ... convenient.'

'Okay,' Boc rubs his hands together. 'So we use these two days to prepare. Sort out our stuff. But no swiping, all right?'

'The minute you do, you'll be back on grid.' Mason turns back to the industrial estate. 'And we don't want any attention before we leave.'

'But what if the police turn up?' I ask. 'They'll be at Echo's place for sure. Probably want to interview Mason's parents.'

'So, we just keep out of sight while they're there,' Mason says simply. 'They think we've jumped, right? So they won't expect to find us. It's like you said, people just see what they expect to see.'

Boc's hand goes to rest on Echo's shoulder. 'Ready?'

'Yeah.' She raises an eyebrow my way as farewell.

They're turning to go when I realise that I know what they're headed into much more clearly than they do. They're so used to everything being offered up to them, they have no idea of the world they're about to face.

Part of me just wants to watch them go, let them find out the hard way. *See how you cope now, Boc.*

But he's with Echo.

Arm outstretched. 'Wait. Before you go, there's stuff you need to know.' They pause and turn back. 'You can't swipe to cross the street like you normally do. Find someone else and follow them, okay?'

They're all quiet now, listening.

'Anything else?' Echo asks.

'Doors. Some of them are just movement sensors but others

are triggered by chips.' My mouth scrunches in apology. 'Don't think you can tell just by looking at them.'

'Great,' says Boc, deadpan. 'No eating. No drinking. No going anywhere. That everything?'

I only manage a hand at the back of my neck. 'Just … don't let anything open for you, and don't expect anything to work. You're as good as illegal for the next two days.'

Boc reacts with a snort when I say that, but I stand my ground. *Now you'll see what it's like.*

He doesn't say anything, just turns away with Echo. They begin down a track towards the old highway.

I'm lifting my hand to say goodbye, when Mason steps closer. 'Come with us.'

My mouth opens then closes again as all my thoughts spin upside down. 'I …' Don't know what to say.

I'm not even sure I could jump that far. But just for a moment, I let myself imagine. Taste the possibility of a future, ten years from now. The pull of the unknown. Even if we found a life that we didn't expect, at least we'd be together.

'Someone once said to me that for all we know there might be any number of possibilities out there.' His voice is low, standing about as close as he could get without actually touching me. '*Unless we can first imagine what might be possible, how will we even know to try? Remember?*'

Of course I remember the words I said on the roof that night, so long ago. Dreaming about going backwards. Time-travelling starlight. The whole world out there, waiting for us. But even as I lean closer and my forearm brushes against the back of his hand, it's as if something is crushing my chest. I'm only able to breathe into the top of my lungs. And I know exactly why.

In another world, some other time, I'd throw my arms around his neck and hold him tight telling him, *yes*. Yes, yes, yes.

'Mason, I … would … love to.'

He can hear it in my voice. 'But?'

'I can't leave Mum.' Head shaking. 'I just … couldn't. I can't …'

'Could you teach her? Wait behind until she's ready, then bunny hop together.'

It makes me smile, his hope, determination. *Imagine if we could* …

Dinging from a railway crossing starts up in the distance, bringing us back. Before we find out what the future holds, we have to deal with the next two days.

He exhales in a rush, stepping back. 'Think about it, yeah?'

I let my chin drop. 'See you in two days.'

CHAPTER TWENTY-TWO

OUR ROOM IS glowing blue from the standby light when I tap on the window at home. Sure didn't need a reminder about how difficult life is without a chip. It's even worse without a compad to make it in via the front door.

A few seconds pass before the top of Mum's face appears over the back of the armchair, a palm rubbing her eye. She slides the window open, blinking through sleep as she guides me inside by one arm.

By the time I've found my feet on the rug, she's blinking through tears. Arms around me, holding me tight, my face pushed against her shoulder and damp now with tears of my own.

'I'm so, so, so sorry.' For causing her worry and for all that has happened. For Amon. And Echo too.

'You're not hurt?' she asks, pulling back only long enough to check my expression.

'No.' But again the tears come, chased by a fresh wave of heartache.

'I thought you'd jumped; I've been checking you on the grid,' she says over my shoulder. 'Saw a news report.'

'What are they saying?'

'He was your friend? Amon Lang. Something about a train. Suspicious circumstances.' Again, she pulls back, this time catching my focus. 'They named Mason, more than once. Put up a photo. Saying that he's a … suspect?'

Fresh tears chase the others. Swallow them down. 'It was an accident. Not Mason's fault, but they're forming a case to convict him. We hacked in to see.'

There's still no space for air in my lungs. Something catches in my throat before I suck for breath again. 'They're planning a big jump. Mason and Boc. Ten years. So far that the case will have closed and he won't be arrested.'

One eyebrow flickers. 'They can go that far?'

'Yeah, pretty sure. Only problem is we don't think it's possible to travel back …'

I'm waiting for Mum to react about Mason and Boc, about travelling ten years into the future, but she rubs her neck. 'Those poor parents. Just awful.'

I lift a hand, keep pushing through. Testing the water, I guess. 'They asked if we want to come.'

There's a pause before her face pinches with disbelief. 'Scout, you can't be serious –'

'You could learn how to jump. I could teach you. We'd still be together.' The words come fast. Have to get them out before she reacts.

We're leaning so close that I can see the raw rims of her eyelids. She shakes her head, just faintly at first but then faster and clearer as her frustration grows. 'No, Scout, no. Absolutely not. That poor boy has *died*.'

My eyes drop. 'Yeah, I know.'

'You have to stop. Do you understand? I mean it this time –'

I should have known.

'I mean it. No more. There's too much at stake.'

'Okay.'

She breaks off, her eyes travelling over my face. Her skin is so pulled and pale. 'How much do they know about you?'

'I don't know. Not much. But I'll deal with any questions.'

'We can't have them watching you, understand?' Mum's eyes are fixed on mine, her eyebrows raised. 'No more. Promise?'

I hate seeing her scared like this. I hold her shoulders, and let my chin drop. 'It's okay, Mum. I promise.'

It's easy this time. I breathe in, deep at last. 'Everything's going to be okay.'

At about eleven thirty on the night they're due to leave, I head down to Footscray Park. Not sure if the others will be there yet, but I want to allow time to say goodbye.

I couldn't risk sending a message, best to stay off-grid these past two days, but I did try to see Mason last night. When I made it to his house, both his parents' smartcars were in the driveway. Lights shone from the middle rooms in the house but the garage was dark. I'm not sure what it was about the cars and the lights exactly, but for a while I just sat on my bike, one foot braced against the driveway as I tried to picture the scene being played out inside. What would they be saying to each other in there? How must it feel for Mason, maybe telling his parents about his plans, preparing them for the next ten years? Or, perhaps worse, not telling them. Maybe leaving a note to explain once he's gone.

In the end, I turned around and rode home. Let him have his last few hours with his family uninterrupted.

A torch is glowing near the cave entrance when I come close, three figures moving around, carrying clear vacuum-sealed bags that look like they're packed with clothes.

One of the figures looks up as I approach. Echo. She manoeuvres her way around the native grasses then just keeps coming, straight into a hug. I'm not ready at first; it's as if I've been hit with a wave of raw emotion. Then again, her brother is dead; this is probably the only way to say hello.

It's a real embrace, warm and tight, and as I hug her back I realise that I need this too. We pull away, still no real need for words.

'Are you jumping?' I ask.

'Yes. Mum and Dad too. We're going to bunny hop together.'

It's her parents, the other people here, I realise with a start. Echo's mum comes over and squeezes my hand so tight in both of hers that I feel the bones crunch; her dad just grunts a hello.

I swallow and say hello too but it sounds hollow. I should say more, but I'm not ready with the right words, so I turn to Echo for help. 'I'm …'

'It's okay.' She squeezes my forearm.

It doesn't make sense to me, why they're jumping; Mason's the only one who has to escape. In the police's eyes, they're the victims. But I guess their whole world just turned upside down. Maybe a trip into new possibility is their way of dealing with all they have lost.

Movement along the path a few metres away makes us all turn and wait until we recognise who's coming. We're nearly there, but still anything could happen.

It's Mason and Boc, carrying bags of stuff. They get hugs from Echo, and from her parents too. The relaxed way they speak together in a bunch gives me the feeling that they know each other well. Soon Mason leaves the huddle and makes his way over to me.

The question is clear in his eyes.

I answer with a single head shake. 'I'm … staying with Mum.' But that's okay. I'm all right with staying.

His eyes close for a moment and his body stills. 'I understand.'

I'm searching for a way into goodbye when he pulls a slip of paper out of his pocket. 'I wanted to message you but I didn't want to risk them seeing, so I wrote it down.'

He holds out the slip. I take it and unfold the paper, tilting it towards the torch so I'm able to make out a name and contact numbers.

'He's a lawyer,' says Mason. 'A friend of our family. I knew you might stay so I asked him to check the file they have on you.'

My eyes lift, not sure how to respond.

Mason shuffles closer. 'They're going to call you in for questioning, but it's all for info on me, all right? Even if they try to spook you, our friend said they have no real case on you.'

'That's … wow. Thanks …'

'He says you don't have to tell them anything. Just play dumb. And if they hold you in for any longer than an hour, call him, yeah?'

I have to ask. 'Does he know about me? Who I –'

'Scout.' His tone is gruff, impatient. 'Get that out of your head, okay? Maybe you were illegal once, but not now.'

It's almost too much. Before I know it I'm flinging my arms around his neck, holding him so tight that I can feel his chest move with each breath. He has me around the waist, my heels lifting off the ground. No words anymore.

We stay that way, holding onto the moment. Frozen in forever.

Too soon our arms loosen and my heels return to the ground. Pulling away slowly, I turn my hand to cup his jaw and leave it there, one last moment together. *Goodbye. Stay safe.*

He lifts his hand to cover mine, tilting his head just enough for his lips to touch my skin, a kiss at the place where my wrist meets the edge of my palm.

Almost as soon as I feel his touch he lets go, already turning away. Because who wants to hold onto this moment? The worst one. The last.

I've been hovering outside the cave for a while when I decide to check. No-one here. Piles of clothes mark the spots where each person once was.

I decided not to watch them jump, choosing to stay outside rather than psych any of them out. Now there's no need to stay, even Echo and her parents don't expect to return for months, but for some reason I hang for a while in my secret refuge. The spring water still tastes achingly cold. My tools and other stuff are still stashed in a corner, but now they have been joined by the vacuum-sealed bags.

The blanket is still there when I examine the ground by the light of the torch, covering the woman who died, decomposed in patches with long shapes of bone underneath.

I guess, knowing now what I do, there probably was someone who missed her once. Maybe she wasn't important to anyone but me the night she died, but there must have been someone who missed her when she first learnt to time skip, someone who cared about her, from another place, another time.

It must be a few hours before dawn when I make my way back, climbing out through the gap in the fence at Footscray Park. I reach Ballarat Road and hover for a while, aware that I'm still blocked from the grid, still invisible as long as I don't swipe.

What shall I do, I ask myself, *with my last few hours of freedom?* What secrets could I explore while I'm still off-grid?

But all I can think about is the people who have left me behind, and the ones still waiting. Mum, Alistair, and even Kessa.

And standing here with the night sky above me, I realise that there's nothing more that I need to do off-grid. Maybe Mason's right; I'm not illegal anymore.

So I make my way to the crossing point, swipe and wait. Not many smartcars around at this time of night but soon I hear the familiar hum dropping in tone as two of them stop.

I make my way across safely, conscious that by triggering the crossing point I'm not blocked anymore. I'm back on the grid again.

When I make it to the other side, I check the slip of paper in my pocket, a new kind of lifeline. It's still there, still safe. All I can do now is wait until the police come. I just have some questions to answer before I make it back to the place where I have rations and a good school. The life of a citizen is waiting for me, just the other side of now.

No police show the following day, or the day after.

After a while I begin to wonder whether they're waiting for Mason to return before they swoop in for questioning. That's fine with me, of course. If they're waiting for any of the others to show, they'll be waiting a long time. Maybe I'm off the hook long-term.

I'm careful not to hack anything, don't even check the grid. My history map over the past couple of days shows the life of a normal citizen. From now on, I'm going to stay way honest and squeaky clean. Once I make it through the questioning,

I'll begin jumping again. For now I live through every moment as if that were the only way to live. I have a wide future waiting, but first I have to play it safe.

It's not long until waiting for the police is replaced by final registration requirements, collecting stationery and finally, the first day of school. It's the day I've always dreamed of, but now that it's here it feels sort of … tainted. The dream isn't how I'd imagined because of the people no longer here.

I meet a few more people and hang out with Kessa, chatting about the teachers we have and stressing about homework. I get to pick electives like food technology and chemistry, the ones that will take me towards my goals.

Sometimes, though, I find myself staring at the crowd lining up for the sensors at the canteen, watching them as if from a distance, through some sort of glass wall.

I'm the only one here who knows that something more is possible. They're living this life only because they have no idea how else they could live. One day I might teach people about time skipping, offer them a future they never realised they could reach. But not yet. First I have to make it through school, secure a place at uni.

For now I need to wait until I'm truly safe, until there's a bigger gap between who I am now and who I used to be.

We're watching the Monday evening news when it happens. Partway through a segment on an attack at the East India border, the sound cuts out and a message flashes on the screen: Entrance Warrant Activated, Federal Police. Mum's barely had a chance to take screen control when we hear the front door release and footsteps along the hall.

After all this time, nearly six weeks since the others left, it's almost a relief. I slip on my boots and find the slip of paper that Mason gave me stashed safely on the bedside table. Let's get this questioning over with.

Mum opens our door as they approach, although I get the feeling they would have disengaged it without waiting for us.

'Coutlyn Roche?' A police officer holding a swipergun steps into the room.

'Yes. That's me.' Two others in bulletproof vests stand just outside the door.

He lifts the swipergun towards my wrist so I hold it out obediently, pulling up my sleeve. The gun lets out three quick beeps.

'I hereby inform you that you are under arrest by order of federal law. Anything you say may be used against you during federal trial –'

'Under arrest?' I pull back my arm, my heart quickening.

'What's going on?' Mum is standing behind the armchair, her hands playing nervously beneath her chin.

The officer clicks a handcuff over my wrist. It gives a ping as it engages. 'I'm sorry to be the bearer of bad news, ma'am, but this kid you're looking after is in possession of a stolen chip.'

'There must be some mistake –' Mum's voice is rushed and high.

'No mistake, ma'am. She's up for fraud, impersonating a citizen, a whole pile of charges. We've been gathering evidence for a while.'

'No but … she's not, not illegal …'

'She's a fraud, ma'am. You've been taken for a ride.' He lifts my wrist to examine the chip scar and my whole world tilts, thoughts running a million directions.

'See?' The officer continues, still holding my wrist. 'They even know how to fade the scar so that you can't tell it's stolen property.'

None of this is happening. It can't be. We're about to finish last night's fruit salad, aren't we? And after that I have a maths assignment to start.

Except, now the officer is pulling my arms behind me, clicking my wrists into handcuffs.

My mind snaps to the slip of paper in my pocket. 'I'd like to call someone.'

'You have a right to an attorney under federal law,' the officer says, monotone. 'However, it is my duty to inform you that once you are recognised as illegal you will no longer be subject to the rights of citizens.'

It's only now, with both hands locked behind my back that I realise how little help the slip of paper is going to be. If I were a real citizen in trouble, Mason's lawyer would be there for me, ready to help. But the minute he's told I'm illegal, everything's going to change. I know how the world works. I can't count on that lawyer any more than I can expect water rations.

My arms get pulled back as the officer jerks on the handcuffs, testing that they're secure. He leans closer to my shoulder, his voice low: 'And before you try any funny business, know that we've worked you out. Try any of your tricks, and the whole area will be secured when you come back. Understand? We know what you can do and we also know that you have to come back to the same place.'

My whole body has turned cold, my heart barely able to beat. This can't be happening. I'm about to be taken into custody, handcuffed and escorted out of our room. From there I'll be taken into a locked van, and then transported to a holding cell.

Once I'm in that cell, time skipping isn't going to save me. Nothing is.

'But there must be a mistake,' Mum's voice is faint. 'She's just a kid …'

'You'll have the opportunity for debriefing later, ma'am.' The officer lifts a mouthpiece under his chin, warning the team that he's about to bring me out.

He's distracted while he waits to hear a response from someone waiting outside, and in those few seconds I realise. This is my chance.

The officer frowns and fiddles with an earpiece as if trying to turn up the volume.

I step away. Another step backwards, towards the fireplace. That's the best bet in here of returning to clear space, the circular row of bricks around the old fireplace. Maybe they'll pull the building down while I'm away, but I'll take my chances. I know what type of future is waiting for me if I stay.

The officer has glanced my way, aware that I've stepped back. But again he's distracted by something being said on the other end. His focus shifts once more as he speaks into the mouthpiece.

One final step and I'm here, standing with my back to the brick fireplace, hands still locked behind me.

My eyes travel across the room to find Mum, her cheeks flushed and her hands clasped in front of her mouth. Her eyes instantly find mine, blinking through tears. So wide, so full of fear.

How badly I have failed her, after all that she's done. Sorry isn't going to cut it for this one.

Her eyebrows lift, a look of desperate hope and love. *Just hold on, we'll get through this.*

But I reply with a shake of my head. *Please understand.*

The officer has finished with the support staff outside. He clicks off the mouthpiece and turns my way.

I'm so, so, so sorry …

Her hands drop and her forehead quivers as she comes to understand. But already the officer is stepping towards me. Can't wait any longer.

I close my eyes, drop my head forwards and plunge deeper into the tunnel than ever before.

Ten years into the future.

Acknowledgements

A mountain of gratitude to Hilary Rogers for her generous support, expert criticism and willingness to take a risk during the development of this book; I'm grateful for every minute. Warm thanks to Natasha Besliev and the rest of the team at Hardie Grant Egmont, especially Niki Horin and Penelope White. I don't make it in to the office very often but your ongoing emails and support is very much appreciated. This book owes a huge debt to the HGE marketing team and to Charlotte Bodman for introducing it to the rest of the world. Thanks also to Karri Hedge for editing the story with such clarity and compassion; a world that felt very real to me is now much more real as a result of you believing in it.

To everyone – family, friends and acquaintances – who asked me how my writing is going: thank you! It might not seem like much, but your question is often just what I needed to keep going. Thanks also to Chrissie Keighery, Sara Gerardi and Claire Saxby for discussions over coffee and peppermint tea about 'all things writing'. One of my favourite things about what we do is the camaraderie and ideas shared with other writers.

To Porter and Elm, thanks for your cheers and understanding during the victories and struggles. And finally, to Campbell: it's been seventeen years and I still miss you if you're gone for just a day. Thank you for sharing the journey with me.

About the author

Thalia Kalkipsakis grew up on a farm on the outskirts of Melbourne with a mum who tried to save battery hens by on-selling them as backyard chickens. Her dad worked as an industrial chemist while also growing strawberries, carrots and Christmas trees on the farm. It was not unusual  to find plant shoots in the freezer, or the hair dryer missing because it was needed to heat one of her dad's experiments. Thalia's childhood showed her the magic that can happen when science and nature combine with human creativity.

In 2012, Thalia released her first standalone young adult novel, *Silhouette*, which follows a talented and determined young dancer as she navigates her way into the adult world of commercial dance.

These days, Thalia lives in regional Victoria with her husband, their two children and two black cats.

www.thaliakalkipsakis.com